UNTIL DEATH

TEMPTING THE FATES BOOK THREE

ALICE WILDE

Print Edition | Until Death by Alice Wilde
©2023 Alice Wilde

This is a work of fiction. Names, places, characters, and incidents are either the product of the author's imagination or are used fictitiously, and any resemblance to any actual persons, living or dead, organizations, events, or locales is entirely coincidental.

For permissions contact:
alicewildeauthor@gmail.com

ISBN: 9798396076853

To love until Death do us part.

CONTENT WARNING

Dear Reader,

Thank you for picking up Until Death, book three in Tempting the Fates. This is a dark, plot-heavy fantasy romance with multiple love interests. Each book will end on a cliffhanger until the series is complete.

Please be aware that this series may not be suitable for all audiences, and it is certainly not for all ages. If you choose to continue, be prepared to encounter some language, mental/physical abuse, murder, suicidal thoughts, kidnapping, violent behaviors, the mention of non-con and attempted non-con (not by the love interests), death, violence, choking, voyeurism, mutilation, monsters, gods, revenge, redemption, heartbreak, and descriptions that may otherwise trigger you.

However, you will also find a great deal of wonderful and strange characters as well as angst, slow burn romance and eventual spice (this is not a fade to black series), and a cast of characters that is met and built slowly over the course of the story. This series is also multiple POV, so please be aware that some chapters may overlap slightly.

All this being said, there may be other triggers within the series that I have not listed. The journey will not be an easy one for our characters, but it'll be worth it in the end.

Or so one can hope.

Shall we begin ... *Tempting the Fates?*

Alice

DEATH

My hands clench into fists at my sides. Pain unlike anything I have ever known claws its way through my chest, threatening to destroy my will to stay where I am.

To obey Hazel's command, despite knowing that my very existence means nothing without her by my side.

My shadows crash around me, unable to hide the tempest raging within my soul as all I ever wanted leaves me behind.

But I stand my ground.

I will *not* go after Eros and Hazel, not before I have evidence of my innocence.

No matter how great my desire is to take her from him and into my own arms once again.

No matter how much it feels like my heart is being torn from me with each added step between us.

No, I will not go after her again until I can prove myself to her. Until she can be made certain that nothing will come between us again.

That I will stop at *nothing* to prove that my love for her is true.

I let out a ragged breath as I swallow the agony at the back of my throat and turn to look toward the gate and the souls beyond. Though my eyes move over them, my thoughts remain fixed on Hazel.

She was right about one thing; her father should not be here.

At least, not so soon.

Perhaps it is for this reason why I let her leave with Eros in the first place. Our deal should have protected him from dying for at least one moon cycle, even if his treacherous wife poisoned him again. Hazel's sacrifice, her strength poured into him, should have been enough to temporarily sustain him against something so trivial.

Unless, it was not mere poison that killed him.

Stepping toward the gate, I watch the wandering souls beyond, and several turn to blink blearily at me. Just as quickly, their interest wanes and they turn away as if they can sense that I am not the keeper of this gate.

I furrow my brow in thought at this.

Though they can obviously sense my presence, they do not otherwise react to it. There is no fear, no desperation, no emotion at all ... not a living body remains among them.

Never, in all my existence, have I seen anything like this. Unless a catastrophe has beset the mortal realm, most should still have some connection to their former selves.

And yet, these souls do not.

My jaw hardens as my eyes narrow on the crowd.

There is something far more sinister at work here than I thought, and I fear this is just the beginning.

Shifting my attention away from the wandering souls, my gaze locks on Hazel's father.

"You," I say, closing the distance between us, "tell me, what happened to you?"

The man's eyes are hollow and lifeless as he looks up at me. Slowly his head tilts to one side, but he remains quiet.

"How is it that you came to be here?" I press.

"Here," Hazel's father repeats, the word a garbled mess as it pushes past his lips. He blinks once, his head lolling to one side as he eyes roll in their sockets.

I let out deep sigh of frustration. There is little point to questioning a man with no answers to give.

Hazel's father has no idea where he is, let alone what happened to him. He is too far gone, the ties between his body and soul severed, for it to have been mere poison that killed him.

Though I am quite certain I know which mortal creature is responsible for his untimely demise, I must find a way to prove to Hazel that I am not the one to blame. That I have kept my word, despite what it may look like.

I must find out how her father ended up here despite her sacrifice, and I will do everything in my power to save him from this fate.

To make sure Hazel's soul was not given in vain.

I must trust that Eros will keep her safe, though the very thought causes bile to rise in my throat. I do not trust him; and yet, I have no choice. This is what she wishes of me, and I must accept it for the time being.

Until I can ease her suffering and quiet her fears once again.

I watch Hazel's father for a moment longer as he slumps against the gate, already having forgotten me in the haze of his current existence.

There is no other choice for me but to go before the Fates themselves. With the gates shut, only they can give me the answers I need, and perhaps the future I so desperately seek to share with Hazel.

I have no doubt they will find a way to use this against me.

My lip curls up in disgust at this, my hands balling into fists at my side as rage and uncertainty war within me. Closing my eyes, I take a deep breath in and exhale slowly.

So be it, I will do whatever it takes to make sure Hazel is given everything she is owed a thousand times over.

Double checking the red ribbon binding Hazel's father to the gate, I turn back to face the Underworld.

And, ultimately, the Fates themselves.

2

HAZEL

Eros is quiet as he walks beside me.

Lost in grief, I barely notice the changing scenery around us as we move. With one arm wrapped around his, and the other still clutching the small package I found on Death, Eros gently guides me through the dark forest.

Though I find our closeness unnerving, as long as our skin does not touch, at least it isn't physically draining as well ... and I'm thankful that I'm not completely on my own at this moment.

Especially given my current state.

Occasionally Eros will softly mutter something, words meant to distract or comfort me I'm sure, but they fall on deaf ears. I am lost in a daze of emotions, unable to even muster a half-hearted mumble in response to him.

It's strange to be walking through the trees like this.

It was just a few days ago that I was here with Death

5

at my side. My heart full of hope, love, and the possibility of a future.

A future with *him.*

I had thought Death was everything I'd ever wanted.

Now it's Eros who leads me back to Aglaia, City of the Gods ... and I can't help but feel like I've made a grave mistake.

Eros keeps me tucked against him as we move deeper into the woods, and I wonder how I allowed myself to end up here.

My heart feels like it's breaking over and over again with each step I take. Not just over the death of my father, but over Death himself.

The loss of him at my side. The loss of my trust in him ... and worst of all, the loss of what could have been.

My love for him is deeper than even I had realized, and it makes what he's done that much more unbearable. His betrayal stings deeper than anything I've felt before.

And yet, part of me still wants nothing more than to turn around and run back to the gates. To throw myself into his arms, allowing him to wrap me up in his icy embrace and wipe away my tears.

More than anything, though, I just want him here by my side. The urge to glance about, seeking him out in the shadows around us, is almost impossible to ignore ... but I do.

I hate the way I hope he's somewhere nearby, watching over me, keeping me safe. Despite everything, I still want him to be close.

But deep down, I know he's not.

I cannot feel him near me. The darkness doesn't hold the same inkiness to them that his shadows do.

There's no chill in the air to reassure me that he's watching, and it's all my fault.

I hate the doubt that creeps into the back of my mind. Perhaps I made a mistake sending him away.

Perhaps ...

I shake my head as I am reminded of my father. Of seeing him here in the Underworld, lost and confused, even after I gave my very soul to save him.

No, I was right to tell Death to stay away.

For what is a man, god or otherwise, worth who cannot keep his word?

Nothing.

At the very least, he is not one I want to be bound to.

If Death cannot prove that he kept our deal, then I don't know how I'll ever be able to trust him again.

After all, he lied about finding my book ... If he is that jealous of another man's love for me, and my *father's* at that, why should I believe he's not lying about our deal, too?

It would do me well to remember *that*, instead of longing for him.

I try my best to let my heart harden against Death. I have tried, for my mother's sake, to remain soft, but where has that led me?

To death.

I will not let love be my downfall, but even as I think this, I know my heart will not listen. I love Death, and I cannot help but hope that he proves me wrong.

Turning, I find Eros' watching me, concern clear on his face, and force a small smile to my lips.

"Thank you for walking with me," I tell him. "I'm not sure I trust these trees."

"And you would be wise not to, they have a way of leading souls astray."

I frown at this.

"And the white creature I saw you transform from, was that a trick of the forest's, too?"

"No," Eros says, nervously clearing his throat. "That was all me, I am afraid."

"Really?"

"Yes, it is one of my many forms," he says, giving me a half-grin. "I thought it would be the fastest way to catch up with you, but I had no intention of startling you into the grasp of the forest."

"How many forms do you have?"

"Ah, now you are finally asking the interesting questions," he says with a delighted laugh. "My dear mortal, I am limitless in what I can become. In fact, I can take on just about any form you desire to see me in."

"*Any* form?"

I try to keep surprise from slipping into my tone as I try to imagine Eros as anything other than himself ... let alone that fearsome beast. Though I suppose at this point, nothing should surprise me.

After all, I am dead ... Little more than a wandering soul myself. One who once kissed Death himself.

"What do you have in mind?"

I bite back my reply, knowing there is still only one being I wish more than all the rest to see.

"Nothing."

"Oh, very well."

"Perhaps the beast from before?" I say quickly, noting the disappointed slump of his shoulders.

Instantly he perks up as if excited to show off another of his powers, and I suspect that's exactly what it is.

"I would be happy to oblige, but you will need to secure that package of yours and climb up onto my back first."

I frown at this before warily asking, "Why?"

His grin widens at my question as he leans in close, and for a moment I'm distracted by his nearness. Eros' beauty is somehow heightened with proximity, not to mention the intoxicating scent of him that now washes over me.

Distantly, I am all too aware that I should be wary of him and his charms.

But with Death no longer here to ground me, I find my self-control around Eros wearing away despite my best efforts.

"I cannot very well lose my hold on you, mortal one," he tells me, his voice low and soft as it trails its way down my spine. "Not within these trees. Besides, this is the only way you will get to meet my beast while remaining perfectly safe by my side."

"Perhaps this isn't such a great idea."

"Come now, I will even allow you to ride me back to the city," Eros says, the corner of his mouth twitching slightly. "Certainly, you cannot say no to an offer like that. Not when I can sense the curiosity burning bright within you."

He pulls back slightly as if to search my face.

It's impossible to miss the mischief in his expression, but I force myself to disregard it. An overwhelming sense of exhaustion has taken root within me, and I quickly realize that I don't want to fight him on this.

"I suppose it would be nice to not have to walk for a moment," I say softly.

"Then it is settled."

Before I have a chance to change my mind, he kneels, his hands sliding down my arms and over the curves of my legs to the very hem of my skirt. Taking the now stained and dirty fabric in both hands, I let out a gasp of surprise as he tears a long slit up one side, freeing my legs from within.

As unrecognizable as the starlight dress had become, given my previous journey through the forest, I'm still sad to see it so utterly destroyed.

"Was that necessary?" I ask, as he rips another strip of fabric from the hem of my dress, catching my hand before I can pull away from his hold on my skirt.

"Yes, it was. Now, take hold of me, and do not let go" he orders. I do as he says, and he carefully pries the small package from me and wraps it in the length of fabric before securing it to my person. "There. Ready?"

Eros doesn't wait for me to respond before he swings me up onto his back, his movements too gentle and quick for me to realize what's happening before it's already done. I don't even get a chance to express my shock and annoyance over being manhandled in such a way before he's shifted beneath me.

Gone is the man I know as Eros, and in his stead now stands a giant white beast. Surprise crashes through me as I clutch at handfuls of his thick fur to keep myself from falling to the ground far below.

He lets out a low growl that rumbles through my body just before he sets off at a pace that leaves me breathless with exhilaration and fear. Wind whips past me, tugging at my hair and dress as he darts around trees, beneath clawing branches, and over giant boulders.

The forest blurs past us, and I press myself flatter against Eros' back, clinging to him with every ounce of strength left in my body. The thrill of riding him soon outweighs the terror, as I watch the world shift around me, knowing that I am safe here atop him.

It's almost enough to make me forget my worries.

Almost.

As we reach the edge of the forest, Eros slows to a gentle trot before stepping out of the tree line. Without warning, he suddenly shifts again, and I let out a squeak of surprise as he twists to catch me. Only he's misjudged my reaction and we end up tumbling to the grass instead.

I let out a grunt as I crash to the ground, my back hitting hard enough to knock the air out of my lungs before he manages to twist me around so that I'm now lying on top of him.

My heart pounds, my chest heaving as I struggle to fill my lungs with air. Eros stares up at me, his own chest rising and falling steadily beneath me.

I know I should remove myself from him, but I find that I am unable to, my body still stunned by the shock of the fall. My cheeks burn as Eros' pale eyes fix on me and he reaches up to cup my face in the palm of his hand.

The touch of his skin pulls at me, begging me to give in to him as it threatens to drain me of myself. Swallowing, I open my mouth to say something, but the words never leave my mouth.

Eros' fingertips dig into my hair as they push their way toward the back of my head, pulling me down to him. His lips find mine, and I'm immediately lost in him as everything else fades. Eros deepens the kiss, searching me, body and soul, as his hunger for me becomes ever more consuming.

My mind reels as I struggle to remember anything else, but all I'm aware of is him, his touch, as my body trembles in want ... in need for more. Sense finally comes crashing back to me as I feel his free hand slip lower on my back. Push my hands firmly against his chest, I break our kiss as I once again gasp for air.

It takes a moment for me to realize what just happened, and I can't help but look away in shame. How easily he seems to weaken me, to break my resolve with nothing more than a kiss.

I should have known better than to let my guard down with Eros ... especially so soon after leaving Death's side.

Guilt pits in my stomach like a sickening weight at the thought of Death and the feelings that still linger for him. Feelings I'm starting to doubt can ever be shaken despite his betrayal.

"I ... I'm sorry," I say to Eros as I remove myself from his body.

"There is nothing to apologize for, mortal," Eros says with a half-grin as he props himself up on his elbows. But even I can see the disappointment hidden behind his expression. "Here, let me help you."

Eros rises to his feet, brushing the dirt and twigs from his dirt-stained suit before offering his hand to me. I stare at his hand warily for a moment, the thought of accepting it suddenly seeming far too dangerous given what just happened.

I'm starting to worry that I can't trust myself around him anymore, not after the way his kiss burned through me, igniting a fire for him that should never have existed in the first place.

Glancing toward the city, I feign absentminded ignorance as I accept his help by grabbing his sleeved arm instead of his hand. I drop my hand from him the moment I'm back on my feet.

"We're nearly there, I think I'd like to walk the rest of the way," I tell Eros as cheerily as I can. "It's not often someone like me can say she walked the streets of the gods."

He nods once, and we continue on in silence toward the city gates.

As we draw nearer, I steal a glance up at him. It's impossible to deny the power he carries in his touch, and I can't help but wonder what giving in to him would be like.

Not that I would allow that to happen, not while I still carry Death so heavily in my heart. If touch had not been so impossible between us, I wonder if I would still feel these baser desires for Eros, too.

Or if I am simply reacting to a need so long left wanting that it's starting to crave even that which it should not. I shift my gaze away from Eros at this, even as the soft morning rays seem to outline him in angelic light.

Thankfully, the moment my bare feet hit the paved roads of the city, I'm distracted from my thoughts by the chaos that rises up to meet us.

Creatures and beings of all kinds move about with a sense of urgency that puts me on edge. Obviously, something has happened since we were last here.

Eros steps closer to me, uncertainty furrowing his brow as he senses the growing confusion all around us.

"Come," he urges, grabbing my hand before I can protest as he quickly moves toward a small lane.

I fight to keep up as his pace quickens, leading me through the twisting back alleys of the city.

"What's happening?" I ask, my voice nearly breathless from exertion.

Eros doesn't answer as he pauses at the end of a narrow path. Spinning around, he shoves me roughly back against the vines of one wall before covering me with his own body.

Eros is quick to press a hand over my mouth to silence my protest just as several giant men race by. His touch has my mind reeling and knees weakening beneath me, his body the only thing keeping me upright at the moment.

We remain like this for a few seconds longer, my heart pounding in my chest, before he finally steps away from me. But before I have a chance to regain clarity, he's grabbed my hand again, dragging me across the open street ahead and into another maze of winding alleys.

I'm nearly stumbling at this point, my body aching in more ways than one.

"We are nearly there," Eros whispers, as if sensing my exhaustion. "Just a few mo—"

He stops short and I slam into the back of him as a pair of stone guards suddenly step into view ahead, blocking our path.

Eros curses under his breath, his fingers tightening on me as I peer out from behind him.

"You, there," one of the guards says, his deep voice rumbling through me, "you are to come with us."

It was Eros they were searching for?

Frowning, I wonder what he's done to have the whole city in such turmoil. Glancing up at him, he gently pushes me further behind him as he attempts to block me from the view of Hades' guards.

Only now does it strike me that they weren't speaking to him, but to me.

"I am afraid you must be mistaken," Eros says as their eyes remain locked on me. "The mortal and I have only just returned to the city and have a pressing matter to attend to. Now, if you will excuse us, we will be on our way."

He attempts to drag me past the guards, but they do not move to let us through.

One places a heavy hand on his shoulder, nearly forcing him to his knees as he staggers under the sudden weight of it.

"It was not a request," the other guard says as their

gaze once more returns to me, and I try my best not to shift uncomfortably beneath it. "By high orders of Hades, all women within the city are to be brought before him. Immediately and without exception."

3

HAZEL

"She is but a mere mortal," Eros scoffs with a dismissing wave of his hand. "Surely, Hades cannot mean her. She is far too common a creature for his tastes—"

His words sting, but the guards are completely indifferent to his comments as they shove him roughly aside and reach for me.

"Come," one of the guards orders even as I shrink away from them, drawing further back between the narrow walls as I glance nervously at Eros.

"Run," the pale god breathes, and it's all I need to hear.

I turn, my aching feet padding against the stone as I race back the way we came. Behind me, I hear one of the guards let out a roar, and the next moment the whole city seems to come alive around me. The earth and walls shake from the echoing chorus of returned voices, nearly sending me crashing to the ground as the vibrations rattle me to my core.

Thankfully, the narrow passageways between the gods' palaces seem to be too small for the likes of Hades' stone guards as I hurtle through them. Still, I dare not glance behind me to check.

Turning a corner, I suddenly slam straight into a hard chest and cry out in panic as arms wrap around me.

"It is only me, mortal," Eros breathes heavily.

"How," I gasp, the single word barely making it past my lips.

"They have no interest in me. It is you they want, hurry. If we can just make it to my bedroom—"

Swallowing, I shake my head, my legs trembling beneath me and finally give out. Eros catches me before my knees can crack against the stone, my body falling limp in his arms.

"I'm sorry," I whisper once my voice has returned to me. "Please, let me stay here and rest a moment."

"I am afraid that is not possible."

"They cannot fit into the alleyways, can they?"

"No, but there are others who can, and they have already summoned them."

My eyes widen in fear as I look up into Eros' face, surprised to find my own trepidation staring back at me.

"What do they want with me?"

"I am afraid I do not have an answer for you," Eros says, but I can tell from the way his jaw clenches that he may know more than he's letting on. "Here, let me carry you."

I don't argue with him as he lifts me up off the stone and into his arms.

"Why not fly us out of here and to your palace?" I ask

quietly after Eros pauses to check our surroundings before rounding a corner.

"There's not enough space to take off, let alone fly safely back from here."

We continue on in silence, Eros' body growing tenser by the minute. It isn't long before I realize why.

The rhythmic march of soldiers' boots thudding against the ground reaches my ears, growing louder and louder as they move toward us.

"Eros?"

Dread fills me as the god's jaw hardens, his Adam's apple bobbing in his throat as we turn to find we've been surrounded on all sides. His white eyes are wide as he whips his head around, backing us up against a wall as well-armed guards fill in around us.

The sound of their footsteps moving in sync suddenly dies out as a tall, broad-shouldered man holds up a hand to signal them to stop. Maddening silence follows for a split second before the man steps forward, his eyes narrowing on Eros before dropping to me.

"Hand the girl over, Eros."

"What does he want with her?"

"That is none of your concern. Do not make this any harder on yourself. We have our orders."

"Deimos, do you honestly think—"

Eros lets out a pained grunt before he can finish his sentence, one of the men standing in the side alley suddenly shoving the butt end of a spear into his side. He stumbles slightly, and another guard takes the opportunity to kick out the back of his legs, forcing Eros to his knees.

I cry out as I fall with him, but somehow, he manages to keep me tucked safely against his chest ... until the point of a black sword is wedged beneath his throat.

"This is your last warning," Deimos says, a cruel grin spreading across his face, "and in all honesty, I would prefer you did not heed it."

"You can have her over my dead—"

"I'll go with you," I say, cutting Eros off before he can finish his threat.

Both men seem taken aback by this as if they'd almost forgotten who they were arguing over.

"You heard the girl," Deimos says, the corner of his mouth lifting as if in challenge.

"Please, Eros," I plead softly against his chest so that only he can hear. "Do not let your blood be spilled here this day. Do not leave me without hope in this place."

Eros only hesitates a second longer before gently setting me down on the ground, the point of the blade unwavering against the bend in his neck. No sooner than I'm out of Eros' arms, then another guard steps forward to yank me to my feet, the thick leather of his glove rubbing roughly against my skin.

"Bring her to the king's palace," Deimos orders, his sword still pointed at Eros as I'm marched away and out of sight of him.

Fear knots my stomach as the last thing I hear from Eros is the echo of a sharp curse.

As we filter out of the narrow alleyways and onto the main road leading up to Hades' palace, it comes as little relief to see that I'm not the only woman being dragged along.

The only thing I can think of that might have brought this about is the ball. But surely, it couldn't be my actions that have warranted this kind of response ... Hades and I barely spoke before Death and I decided to slip away.

No, something must have happened after I left.

My mind, though exhausted, is racing by the time we reach Hades' palace. The halls are swarming with guards and women, the angry shouts of the city's men echoing off the crystalline walls as we're herded further inside.

The other women look just as panicked as I feel, and I force myself to swallow past the worry tightening my throat as we're driven into the throne room. Unceremoniously, the guards dragging me toss me to the floor next to a small group of women. They do nothing but watch as I wearily push myself up onto my feet, each looking just as lost and afraid as I feel.

Stepping toward them I try to meet their eyes, but they quickly look away. The room continues to fill with more and more women, each nervously glancing toward the empty throne.

As crowded as it is, the room is unnaturally quiet compared to the shouts still echoing through the halls toward us.

"Why are we here?" I ask.

"Silence, woman," a guard orders, fixing me with a hard look.

Heat burns my cheeks as heads turn my way, and I bite my tongue, dropping my eyes to the floor, not wanting to draw any more attention than necessary. After a moment, my presence is all but forgotten, and I lift my gaze to peer about the room once again.

It's clear that no one seems to know why we're here, though the unease filling the room is almost sickening in its intensity. A large man pushes past me, nearly sending me tumbling to the floor again as he forces his way through the ever-growing throng of women toward the front of the room.

As I straighten to glare at him, I suddenly recognize him as Deimos. Quickly turning back toward the palace halls, I anxiously search for any sign of Eros ... only to watch in dismay as the heavy doors to the throne room are pulled shut, trapping us inside.

The unnerving silence suddenly turns deafening as the atmosphere in the room shifts, and I slowly turn to watch as Hades enters from a door cut into the stone that I hadn't noticed before.

He moves to stand next to his throne, his eyes trailing languidly over the crowd before him.

My heart skips a beat in my chest as his gaze lands on me, and I'm suddenly terrified that he will recognize me from the night before. After all, I am still wearing the same dress, as unrecognizable as it may be now that it hangs in stained tatters from my body.

A moment passes but then his eyes shift away from me, no sign of recognition within them. I let out a small sigh of relief at this, whispering a silent prayer of thanks to whichever god chose to spare me at this moment.

Though, perhaps it was not the gods, but merely my current state that truly saved me.

"There is a traitor among you," Hades says, his low voice breaking the silence and sending a chill racing across my skin. His words carry a deadly weight to them as he scans the room, those around me hardly daring to breathe, let alone speak as they wait for him to continue. "A woman who has the audacity to try to refuse my orders. To defy me, your king. Your *god*."

The room fills with the soft murmur of whispering voices at this. Try as I might, I am unable to ignore the questions and sharp words that drift about the crowded room as Hades moves to sit on his throne.

"A traitor?"

"What did she do?"

"Where is Persephone? Has something happened to her?"

"Who would dare try to defy Hades?"

"If I learn who the whore is, I will cut her down myself for spoiling my day."

"I bet it was that minx who danced with him at the ball, I saw the way she looked at him."

"It would be one thing if he went after her, but the other way around?"

"Can you imagine? And in front of the queen, too."

Their words fill me with a growing sense of dread, reawakening my fear from earlier ... that is me whom Hades is searching for. The one who caught his eye and then dared to run away instead of following through with our plan.

Realizing this, I take a small step back in an effort to disappear into the crowd around me.

"Den of vipers," a woman with long red hair hisses back at them, surprising me, "to turn on one of your own so quickly, when you well know Hades' own appetites are almost certainly to be blamed."

"You would all be wise to hold your tongues," another woman says, suddenly appearing in the midst of them, "lest you too be found guilty of treachery."

This only seems to have the opposite effect on the crowd though, as the whispers swell to fill the room.

"Silence," Hades roars, rising from his throne, impatience clear in both his tone and expression despite the distance between us. Immediately the room stills, and I fix my eyes on the floor as his own scan the room again. "If the woman has any sense left in her at all, she will step forward now and declare herself."

There's a pause as the others look around nervously at each other, but of course, no one steps forward.

"That was an order!" Hades shouts, startling me into glancing up at him, his lip curling up over his teeth in a snarl.

His eyes flash dangerously, and I realize he's probably not used to being denied what he wants ... and right now, unless I am gravely mistaken, what he wants is me.

Hades' eyes grow darker, his frustration growing, when again no one steps forward. My hands grow slick with sweat as I take another step back, hoping to hide myself from the king's gaze.

I don't know what to do.

Should I risk stepping forward? Would he recognize me if I did?

I'm not even certain that I'm the woman he's searching for, though I can't shake the nagging suspicion that I am. What does he plan to do to me if I am?

This thought alone is enough to have me desperately glancing about the throne room for some way to escape.

Perhaps, if no one steps forward, this will all be over soon. Surely, he can't mean to keep us all here.

As if reading my mind, blue flames begin to lick the edges of Hades' head and shoulders, his rage burning hotter with each passing second.

"As this woman has chosen yet again to defy me, I have no choice but to take matters into my own hands," Hades growls. "You, guard, bring me a stool."

We all watch nervously as a simple stool is quickly found and placed before Hades. His eyes trail over us before stopping on a tall blonde standing off to one side.

With a small nod of his head, two guards step out of the crowd to grab her, dragging her forward as she cries out in surprise.

"My king, please, it was not me—"

"Silence!" Hades orders, causing the woman to flinch as her mouth snaps shut.

My heart thuds in my chest as she is forced down onto the stool, her eyes wide with fear as Hades motions to another guard. He quickly moves to approach the throne, a black box carried in his arms.

Stopping before the throne, I watch with bated breath as Hades lifts the lid and reaches inside. Suddenly, all hope shatters within my chest, horror rushing in to fill its stead as Hades pulls out a single, opalescent shoe.

There is no doubt left in my mind. I am the woman he's looking for.

The traitor to the crown.

My mouth dry, I realize I should step forward, but I remain frozen in place as Hades hands the shoe to the first guard and orders the woman to try it on.

Kneeling, the man obeys, pulling off the woman's shoe before slipping the crystal heel over her foot.

But it doesn't fit.

Hades lets out a low growl of annoyance before waving toward one side of the room. "Clear that side of the room and put her over there. Next."

Instantly, the guards surround the rest of us, pushing us unceremoniously toward the opposite side of the throne room as they form a line down the center of the room to separate us.

Another woman is pulled forward from the crowd and thrust down onto the stool, her own shoe tossed aside as the guard slips the sparkling heel on.

This time, the shoe fits.

"Hmm," Hades murmurs in obvious approval. "Good, place her up against that wall and continue dealing with the rest as such."

His men are quick to obey, and in a matter of seconds, I find myself crushed between the other women in the center of the room, surrounded by guards as two groups begin to form on either side of us.

Those the shoe fits, and those it does not.

It doesn't take long for everyone to realize which side Hades is more pleased with, and soon the women are trying to force their feet to fit. Some going so far as to cause injury to themselves in the process.

I grimace as one such woman screams out in dismay as the heel is wrenched from her foot and she's tossed among those that the shoe does not fit.

"But it fits! I was almost able to—"

A heavy-handed slap from the nearest guard silences

her as she's sent sprawling to the floor before she can clamber back toward the stool. "You had your turn—"

"If she says it fits, let her prove it," Hades says coolly, interrupting the guard.

"Of course, my king."

The woman's tear-stained face brightens as the guard steps aside and she scrambles back to the stool. Taking the heel, she tries her best to shove her foot back inside, her face screwed up in pain as Hades watches from above.

"Did you not say the shoe fit?" he asks, his voice low and dangerous.

"It does, I—"

Kneeling, Hades holds out his hand.

"Give me your foot."

She hesitates for a split second before doing as he asks. The king eyes it for a moment before cupping his other hand around her toes.

The next thing I know, I'm forced to close my eyes as the woman screams out in agony, the crunch of bones sickening as it fills my ears. Another cry of anguish fills the room as her foot is forced into the shoe.

"You are right, the shoe does fit," Hades sneers, motioning for the guard still holding the black box to step closer, "However, as is usually the case, this comes in a pair. Shall we see if the other one fits as well?"

The woman's face pales at this and she quickly shakes her head.

"No, Your Majesty," she says weakly. "I am afraid my other foot is ... is not small enough to fit."

"Such a shame," Hades says with a look of disgust,

returning the second shoe to the box as he straightens. "Very well. Guards, you may carry on."

Hades moves to settle onto his throne, and the woman lets out a nauseating wail as the heel is removed from her broken foot and she's once again dragged away from the stool.

The remaining women quietly try on the heel in turn, accepting their fate without question as they're moved to either side of the room. All too quickly, it's my turn to try the shoes on.

My heart pounds in my chest as I am pulled forward, my eyes momentarily lifting to meet Hades' as he leans against the arm of his throne, his chin propped up by one hand. For a split second, I swear I see the corner of his mouth turn up slightly as if he already knows what my outcome will be.

The guard turns me around, pushing me down onto the stool as the other guard grabs my ankle, scowling in disgust at the sheer state of my feet. I barely have enough time to clutch the sides of the stool for balance before he has lifted my foot off the ground and slipped it into the crystal shoe.

It's a perfect fit, of course.

A second is all it takes for my fate to be decided as I'm dragged off the stool and tossed among the others who also fit the heel. As the last woman is sorted, Hades rises once again to glance between us before waving a hand toward the other, decidedly larger, group of women.

"Release them," Hades says, a ripple of whispered surprise rushing through the others, and I watch in dismay as they're escorted out of the throne room. "As for the rest ... Deimos, have them taken to the dungeons and see to it that they are dealt with properly. Perhaps a night or two down there will teach them better than to test my patience in the days to come."

"Of course, my king," Deimos says with a cruel grin, signaling for his men to act.

The guards step forward, emotionless in their obedience to the king. Panic begins to fill the room as several of the women cry out in fear, heads whipping about in search of a way out, while still others can do nothing but tremble at the thought of what awaits us in the dungeons.

I have to do something.

After all, it is my fault that these women are here. I should have stepped forward earlier and spared the others this fate.

Closing my eyes, I take a deep, steadying breath even as the chaos around me fills my ears. Opening them, I push forward, fixing my gaze on Hades.

"That will not be necessary," I say, my voice just barely rising above the cries of the women as the guards attempt to herd us from the room. "I am the woman you are searching for!"

Almost instantly, my words cause silence to settle over the room once more. Those around me quickly draw back to leave me standing alone in the midst of the crowd.

Hades' gaze falls on me, his expression hard but unreadable in its intensity. All too slowly, he takes a step toward me. His eyes search my face before dropping to rake over my body.

Finally, he shakes his head, and I realize then that he's

not going to accept my confession. Either I'm too late in my admission, or he truly doesn't believe that I'm the one he's after.

"No, girl," he finally says. "You may be brave ... or perhaps *stupid* enough to try to save yourself and the others from this fate, but it is too late."

"I am her. The others need not pay for what I have done."

"Your penchant for self-sacrifice is noted. Though, is your sacrifice truly worth anything when others have already had to pay for your disobedience? When you chose not to step forward when I demanded you do so?"

Frustration and shame war within me as I stare up at him.

He's right, I should have stepped forward the moment I realized I was the one he was looking for. I shouldn't have allowed my own fear to put the others in danger.

Now, I don't know how I'm supposed to prove to him that, despite my actions and ragged appearance, I am the one he's searching for.

"Let me prove it to you," I finally say, though I have no idea how I'll do that.

Hades' eyes never leave my face, and I force myself to meet his gaze.

After a moment, he cocks his head.

"You will have your chance, as will the others," he says. "After all, it is not punishment alone that awaits the woman I am searching for, but a king's reward."

"Reward?"

A murmur of unexpected surprise ripples through the room.

"Yes, a reward," Hades repeats, his eyes lifting from me to look over the other women, "and I can assure you it will be a prize fit for a queen."

Again, many of the women whisper in excitement at this, as if somehow a prize can make up for what he's done to us ... For whatever he plans to do to us.

"Still, I suppose I should also reward one so willing to sacrifice herself to me," Hades continues, his eyes finding me again. "So, I will hold off on sending you all to the dungeons, for now."

Sighs of relief fill the room, but I know better than to let down my guard just yet. After all, Hades did not say he was letting us go.

"Deimos," Hades says, waving a hand, "take the women to the servants' quarters."

Whispers and cries of despair fill the room as the guards once more step forward to usher everyone out. Hades is still watching me, and I force myself to stay rooted to the spot, despite how desperately I want to blend into the crowd.

"Except for this one. This one is to have her own room," Hades tells Deimos. "Put her in the tower, away from the others."

"Yes, my king," Deimos says with a smirk that has me thinking the tower is the last place I want to be kept.

4

E R O S

"Halt, stop right there," one of the guards standing outside Hades' palace orders, blocking my path. "Entry into the palace is currently forbidden."

"Let me through, I have business with the king."

"Then you must wait."

"I am a *god*, or have you forgotten your place?" I hiss.

"These are the king's orders. There will be no exceptions. *Lesser* gods or otherwise."

"You will step aside—"

A grunt escapes me as the other stone guard steps forward and shoves a powerful palm into my chest, forcing me several steps back and away from the main doors.

"You are to wait outside with the others," he says, his voice low and threatening. "However, if you continue to insist upon waiting inside, we will be more than happy to have a cell prepared for you in the dungeons."

Straightening, I brush myself off before giving them

both a hard look, despite being unable to see or sense how it affects them.

The stone guards are notorious for blindly following through with Hades' orders, not to mention their own threats, and the last thing Hazel needs right now is for me to be imprisoned. It would appear that I have little choice but to do as they say, for the time being.

"Fine, but do not think I will forget this abuse of power."

Running a hand through my hair, I turn back to face the crowded courtyard. The space is full of beings of all kinds, though it is impossible not to notice the complete lack of women among them. The very air is different, imbalanced and teetering on the edge of madness as their rage grows with each passing second.

"Tell us what is happening!" shouts one man.

"Where is my wife?"

"Give us back our women!"

"Enough!" roars out a new voice, and I turn to watch as one of Deimos' men emerges from the palace, the two stone guards stepping aside to give him passage. "*Your* women? Do you dare defy your king by declaring ownership over what he may rightfully claim as his?"

A tense silence falls over the courtyard, and I can sense more than a few men bristling at the guard's words. The man seems to realize he has crossed into treacherous waters as he quickly clears his throat.

"Nevertheless, the king, in all his mercy, has chosen to return these to you."

Moving to one side, he signals to another guard.

Within seconds, a flood of women comes pouring out of the palace, eager to be reunited with their loved ones.

I remain rooted to my spot, waiting, hoping to feel the girl's presence, but it is not until the palace doors slam shut that I realize the mortal girl is not among them ... And gathering from the shouts of anger around me, she is not the only one still missing.

Several men stupidly make a rush for the guards only to be cast aside as if they were nothing more than ragdolls.

My own beast might be able to take on the two guards, but there are far too many within the palace walls for me to deal with alone.

Not to mention Hades himself, and the deal he made with the Fates.

"Go home," one of the stone guards roars to the rest of us, "there will be no further entry into the palace today."

I linger for a moment, unwilling to leave the mortal alone here, before finally turning and allowing myself to get swept away with the retreating crowd. I have no choice, not if I wish to be of any real use to her.

My steps are heavy as I move toward my own palace. As I step into the familiar halls, I pass by a room full of naked and writhing bodies finding pleasure in one another, but it does little more than disgust me.

With an exhale of frustration, I slam the doors to the room shut and move deeper into my palace.

It is becoming clearer by the moment that I will not find comfort here.

No, there will be no pleasure to be had until the mortal is safe again.

Not while the girl is held prisoner within Hades' walls, and I am to blame for not protecting her.

As I pace the halls, I nearly trip over a man, my own anger having blinded me to his quiet presence.

"I am sorry, my lord," he says, pulling himself up onto his feet, and my annoyance softens as I feel the man's misery crash over me.

"You are one of my court, are you not? What troubles you?" I ask. "It is not often that I find one so dejected with the walls of my own palace, let alone my very presence."

"Yes, my lord. Please, forgive me," the man answers. "I mean nothing by it. I ... I just cannot stop worrying about my wife."

"Your wife, where is she?"

"The guards took Lilia from me earlier this morning, and she has yet to return."

"And they did not tell you why?"

"No, my lord, but," he pauses, as if unsure whether or not to continue.

"But?"

"May I speak freely?"

"Of course."

"My sister belongs to Hades' court," the man says carefully, "and she mentioned that Hades is searching for one of the women from the ball last night."

"There were a great many women there, all masked. How does he expect to find the one he is looking for?" I mutter to myself.

"I don't know," he answers. "However, I do know it

35

cannot be my wife he searches for. We did not attend the ball, my lord, and she did not leave my side the entire night. And yet, he has not returned her to me."

"Your wife is not the only one being held within Hades' palace."

"But why?"

"That, I am afraid, I do not know."

A choked sob escapes the man at this, and I cannot escape the pain of his shattering heart as it breaks around me.

"My lord, my wife, she is with child. I fear she will lose it if she is not returned to me soon."

I run a hand over my face, letting out a deep sigh at this. I cannot shake the icy dread that drips down my back at his words.

So, Hades is searching for a mysterious woman from the ball, which I am now certain must be the mortal. It was impossible not to taste the lust he felt for her hanging in the air between them last night.

I shake the memory from my mind even as it coats my tongue. I do not wish to imagine what he intends to do with her once he singles her out, if he has not done so already ...

However, knowing Hades, I would not be surprised if he intends to make a game out of wearing her down and, eventually, conquering her.

Especially now that I realize there are others held prisoner with her whom Hades must know are not the woman he seeks.

My stomach twists within me at the thought, and I am startled at the strangeness of the emotion that accompanies it. Disgust, rage, and worry all seem to mix together as I try not to imagine Hades with the girl.

Forcing this unusual feeling aside, I return my focus to the man.

"I will do everything in my power to get your wife and unborn child home safely to you," I say. "You have my word."

"Oh, thank you, Lord Eros. Thank you!"

Leaving the man standing in the hall, I continue on toward the gardens in the hopes of clearing my head as I try to come up with a plan.

Pushing my way through a heavy, flowering vine, I step into a quiet clearing centered around an intricate fountain. Settling onto the stone edge, I am unable to shake the weight that has settled over my shoulders.

Not even the gentle bubbling of the water or the soft floral scent tinting the air seem capable of bringing me any peace. My mind is a tangled mess as it replays the day's events, not to mention what might be happening to the mortal at this very moment.

I am overcome with shame, humiliated that I was incapable of protecting her from Hades and his men. That she is now trapped within his palace walls with no one to defend her.

I have failed, and I have no idea how to go about saving her.

"Eros?"

Half distracted I turn toward the sound of my name. The soft allure of it is more than enough to suggest that whoever approaches means to seduce me.

Despite the all-too-tempting promise of distraction, I find myself furious at the thought.

No, there is no creature within all the realms that could give me the kind of pleasure I seek right now. Not while the only one I truly desire remains Hades' captive.

"I have been looking for you," she purrs. "Come, let us take your mind off your troubles."

Just the mere thought of what she means by her words has my lip curling up in disgust.

How is it that they care about such things at a time like this? Even as I think this, I realize it was only days ago that I would have acted the same way.

"No," I tell her, my voice coming out even icier than I had intended it to.

But she does not seem, or perhaps care, to catch on as she presses, "The whole palace is unsettled, my lord. If we cannot return you to a state of pleasure, no one will be able to find satisfaction within these walls. Please, let us show you all that we've learned while at your court. My sisters and I are quite experienced now."

"Is that it?" I spit. "You seek me out simply to satisfy your own lust? Do you care so little about those around you that you would put your pleasure before another's well-being?"

"My lord?"

"Leave me."

"Eros ..."

"I told you to leave me!" I roar, rising to my feet as anger burns through me, my wings unfurling and causing a gust of wind to whip about the clearing. "Get out of my palace, the lot of you. I will have no one but my own court left within these walls."

Her stunned silence lasts a moment longer before her sob fills the garden.

Immediately my fury abates, but it is too late as I listen to her retreating footsteps as she hurries from the garden.

Letting out a shout of frustration, I sink to my knees. I do not understand what has come over me. I am not one to reprove someone for seeking pleasure from me, let alone lost my temper in such a way over it.

I am losing control over myself, and I cannot help but wonder if my worry over the mortal's well-being is getting to me. Even now, as my head spins, she is the one constant thought that remains.

I feel lost ... starved without her by my side. Just knowing she is out of my reach is tearing me apart from the inside out, and I cannot stand the thought that her absence may stretch on indefinitely.

Let alone that she is lost to the confines of Hades' palace, the last place I would wish anyone to find themselves held captive. The unwelcome thought of her being forced to find refuge in the king's arms wheedles its way into my mind, making my stomach twist.

No, I would be a fool to think she would fall for Hades so easily. Hell, even I could not compel her to fall for me, and I am the very *God* of Lust and Desire.

Enough of these ridiculous thoughts, I simply need to think of a plan to rescue her.

My mind continues to spin before finally landing on my brother, Anteros.

Perhaps I can go to him for help. After all, he still owes me for allowing him to take up so much time in my own, far more pleasurable, palace.

With Anteros' help, not even Hades has the power to keep two lovers apart.

I frown as I let this thought settle in, hope dying in my chest.

Love.

My brother deals in love, and true love at that.

It suddenly seems impossible to seek his help.

After all, love is not what I dabble in. No, that is my brother's business ... one that I have never understood nor wanted anything to do with.

And yet, I cannot shake the thought that when it comes to the mortal, I might be starting to understand.

Pressing a hand to my chest, I realize that I am lying to myself. I cannot begin to understand or explain the feelings I have for her. I crave her with every fiber of my being; yes, but I cannot claim that it is love.

Besides, I do not know what she feels for me, and if my brother is to become involved, I must be certain. Otherwise, we may end up in far more trouble than we are now.

As much as I hate to admit it, there is only one being left whom I can turn to. The only one I know who will do whatever it takes to save her, no matter the cost.

I have no choice.

I must find Death before it is too late.

5

HAZEL

The guards herd us out of the throne room and through the palace until Deimos stops and orders one of his men to pull me aside. I watch the others continue on without me, flinching as several women shoot dark looks my way.

As soon as they're out of sight, I'm led through a series of hallways until we reach a spiraling staircase. I pause, hesitant to start the climb up into the tower.

"Move, girl, before I make you," Deimos growls into my ear from behind, and I hurry to obey.

We ascend for what feels like an eternity before finally reaching a black door at the top of the tower. The guard opens the door as Deimos shoves me roughly forward into the room beyond.

Before I've even had a chance to catch my balance, the room is filled with the sound of a key turning in the lock, and I am officially made a prisoner.

Though the room is far from being a dungeon cell, everything about it is a reminder of where I am.

Of who has taken me captive.

The dark furniture is trimmed in silver and upholstered in deep blue velvets and silks, every bit as beautiful as they are cold and uninviting. Black curtains frame a large, single window that looks out over the world far below.

As much as I hate to admit it, this room is exactly what I expected Death's home to be ... and yet, even his palace held more hope, more warmth in it than this.

Again, I feel the bitterness of regret well up in me at the thought before pushing it aside.

Slowly, I walk toward the large window and push on the glass to open it. Peering out over the edge, I take in the great height of the tower room I now find myself in as I look out over an unfamiliar landscape. Leaning out as far as I dare, I just manage to catch sight of part of the city to my right.

One thing is for sure, there will be no escaping from this window unless I mean to fall to my death.

Sighing, I pull the window shut and turn back to face the room. A flat wall cuts the room in two, a small fireplace set in the middle of it, and a single arched doorway cut into one side. Crossing over, I poke my head through the doorless frame to find a small bathroom on the other side.

Though the room is far grander than anything I had back home, it is a far cry from the rooms I had in Death and Eros' palaces.

Settling onto the edge of the bed, I force myself to come to terms with the fact that I am no guest here.

In some ways, this tower is truly no better than a dungeon cell ... and in the ways that count, it is far worse.

I am being kept alone in a high tower with only one means of entry; a locked door.

There is no possibility of escape.

Certainly not on my own, and those who might wish to help me cannot be expected to know I am here. At least in the dungeons, or with the others, I might stand a chance of being found.

Though, after the looks some of the women gave me, I'm not sure I'd be alive by then anyway. Perhaps I should be thankful I wasn't left alone with them.

Standing, I cross my arms over my chest as I take another look about the room. I wonder how much time I'm expected to spend here, or if Hades will call on me before too long.

My stomach knots sickeningly at the thought, and yet, I know it's inevitable. As is his eventual recognition of me ... even if I have to be the one to remind him.

Guilt weighs heavily on me as I am reminded of what my inaction has led to for the other women stuck here with me. Though, I suppose I cannot be certain he would have accepted my confession had I spoken up sooner.

After all, he didn't seem to believe me when I finally found the courage to step forward.

Rising, I slip into the small bathroom to take a look at my reflection, and I'm mortified by what I find.

Perhaps Hades isn't the one to be blamed for not believing me.

I look nothing like I did last night. My hair is a tangled

mess as it falls in wild half-tied up waves down my back. Twigs and leaves stick out from odd places, and more than a little mud is smeared across my nose and cheeks.

The once-beautiful starlight dress is torn and dirtied beyond recognition, looking more like the brown dress Merelda gave me than one fit for a ball.

It is absolutely no wonder Hades didn't recognize me.

Exhaustion pulls at me as if triggered by a reminder of everything I've been through since yesterday.

Still, I think I should start by cleaning myself up a bit before crawling into bed, regardless of how tired I may be. Besides, it's the very least I should do before Hades sees me next.

My effort may all be for naught, but perhaps if I can prove to him that I am the woman he seeks, Hades may allow the others to leave. Though I am starting to worry it'll take more than a comb and a bit of soap to convince him.

Pushing away from the mirror, I leave the bathroom and cross to a small wardrobe I noticed earlier. Throwing it open, I hold my breath as I peer inside. Thankfully, there are several clean garments hung inside.

All of a sapphire blue so deep, it's nearly black.

Pulling one of the dresses out, I frown at the dark lengths of silk before laying it across the bed to figure out later. It'll have to do, at least I'll have something clean to wear after I bathe.

Returning to the bathroom to draw myself a bath, I'm surprised to find one has already been drawn for me.

Frowning, I glance nervously around the room before stepping closer, only to quickly realize my mistake.

A gentle stream of steaming water flows down one side of the wall into a large basin carved out of the same deep sapphire stone. The water neither overflowing nor draining too quickly to be of use.

As I peel what's left of the ruined dress from my body, I can't help but stare at the tattered and stained rag it's become. Now, it is nothing more than a painful memory of the night before, and the consequences of my own actions.

Hurriedly crumpling the tattered remains, I toss them into the far corner of the room before climbing into the bath. The water is just hot enough not to burn, and a sigh escapes me as I sink deeper into the warmth, letting it lap at my skin as it softens dirt and grime still staining my skin from my night spent in the forest.

Part of me wants to wash the filth off as quickly as I can and slip into bed ... But the rest of me wants nothing more than to linger in the hot water, allowing myself to momentarily drift away from the rest of my problems.

So, that's exactly what I do.

Fully submerging my body in the warm water, I lean back against the edge of the tub. As I close my eyes, I let my mind wander to my father and everything that's happened.

My heart hurts knowing that despite everything I've done, he's dead. I will never again be wrapped safely in his arms or sit by his side while he works, his kind voice offering gentle praise while I practice my own art.

Unless Death can fix this.

As much as my heart aches for my father, it still longs for me to be wrong about Death. For him to prove that this hasn't all just been some great big lie to steal both our souls.

That he truly loves me.

He means more to me than I want to admit, and I worry that my feelings have blinded me to the truth. Perhaps I never should have trusted him in the first place, he is, after all, *literally* death.

Perhaps I should have realized it was all too good to be true.

That *he* was too good to be true.

Allowing Death to be the keeper of my father's soul, as well as my own, was a foolish mistake.

And yet, I truly thought he would be able to save us from our fates.

Apparently, I was wrong.

Tears sting the backs of my eyes as I continue to soak, the water never cooling. It hurts to think that my feelings for Death have been built on a lie. And yet, my heart refuses to let go. Refuses to be convinced of Death's betrayal as it continues to long for him.

Unable to help myself, I let the tears stream down over my cheeks as I quietly mourn the loss of both my father and Death.

After a few minutes, I open my eyes and wipe away the tears.

That's more than enough self-pity for one day. It's my fault that I'm here, and crying over a broken heart isn't going to fix anything.

Regardless of whether or not Death finds a way to save my father, right now, I need to come up with a plan of my own. A way to save my father's soul, if not my own as well.

Letting a hand drift through the wafting steam that curls up over the water, I try to think of some way out of this.

But it all seems so hopeless.

Aside from the stories I've read, I don't know the first thing about the Underworld or the beings that call this place home ... Let alone the rules they live by.

Without Eros or Death, I never would have made it this far. Though, now that I'm Hades' prisoner, I'm not sure that's saying much.

Hades.

As much as I want to escape him, he may be my only way out. He is the king of the Underworld, after all.

Somehow, I managed to capture his attention at the ball. Perhaps I can use his desire for me to my advantage ... if I can convince him that I'm the one he's searching for, that is.

Hopefully, then, I can find a way to persuade him to save my father's soul, or if all else fails, to allow him to stay here with me instead of passing on to the afterlife. As much as I hate to admit it, the longer I consider my current situation, the more I realize that winning Hades to my side may be my best bet.

And in order to do that, I must first prove myself to him.

To make him see that I'm the one he wants.

6

HADES

"The women have been secured in their quarters, Your Majesty."

I continue to stare at the crystal shoe in silence for another moment as I hold it up to the light.

"Good," I say, setting the shoe down in its box before I turn to look at Deimos, "and the girl?"

"Locked away in the tower, as requested."

"Mmm, and what of my wife?"

"She has not left her room since last night, my king."

"Is that so?" I snort.

"Yes, would you like me to have her sent for?"

I mull the question over in my mind for a moment before shaking my head.

"No, in fact, have her doors barred for the time being."

"Your Majesty?"

"Until further notice, I want no one in or out of the palace without my express permission, is that understood?"

"Of course."

"Tonight, the women are to eat dinner with me in the main dining hall. Assign maids to tend to the ones being kept downstairs, and be sure to supply them with whatever they require."

"And what of the girl in the tower?"

"She is to be left alone. Have her brought down to the dining hall after all the others have been seated."

"Yes, my king. Is that all?"

"For now," I answer, "but have Eris brought to me, I have business to discuss with her."

"At once, my king."

Deimos bows deeply before taking his leave, leaving me alone with my thoughts.

Turning back to the crystal shoes, I run my fingertips over them before finally closing the lid.

I move to stand by the window, hoping to distract myself as I look out over the city below, but I cannot help but replay the events of last night over and over again in my mind. The way the girl had looked at me, with her big doe-like eyes and trembling lips, had stirred something deep within me.

A hunger that, until last night, I had thought was long since dead.

But I cannot yet allow myself to be distracted by her, I have a kingdom to rule, and a wife to be brought to heel.

Still, as I wait for Eris to arrive, my mind wanders back to the girl.

I knew from the moment I laid eyes on her that she had no carnal interest in me, despite her less-than-subtle attempts to capture my attention. No, the girl did not want to seduce me ... she had to.

And yet, she chose not to.

Perhaps that is why I find myself so drawn to her.

Despite whatever it was she had been taught to do; I saw the innocence in her eyes and in the nervousness of her touch. And it made me wonder what it would feel like to corrupt her, to mold her, to make her mine in every sense of the word.

A shiver of pleasure runs down my spine at this, just as the sound of the door opening interrupts my thoughts.

I turn to watch as one of my guards shoves Eris inside, ever the stubborn creature.

"Your Majesty," she sneers with a mock bow. "You summoned me?"

"Yes," I reply, turning away from her. "I have a very special task for you tonight, but this time ... it involves my wife."

Eris raises an eyebrow at my words, a smirk forming on her lips.

"Oh? And what might that be?" she asks, sauntering closer to me.

I turn to face her again, my eyes narrowing. "Do not play coy with me, Eris. You know exactly what I want from you."

She chuckles, pressing a hand to my chest. "And what is in it for me?"

I grab her wrist, pulling her hand away from me roughly. "You know what is in it for you. The same thing that has always been in it for you—power, pleasure, and the promise of more to come."

Eris smirks again, pulling her hand out of my grasp and taking a step back. "Very well, my king. What is it you require of me?"

"To do what you do best," I answer. "Sow discord."

7

DEATH

Hours have passed since I left the gates far behind me, moving ever deeper into the dark heart of the Underworld.

My heart is heavy as my feet carry me onward, lost in thought over Hazel and the death of her father. With the gates sealed and her father none the wiser as to how he got here, I cannot be certain that I will find the answers I seek.

Or that those who have them will be willing to give them to me without exacting a heavy price.

But I have to try, for Hazel's sake.

I stop, my shadows swirling up in disgust as a bird calls out from somewhere above, the very trees suddenly shifting around me.

The next moment, the ground beneath my feet comes to life, and I watch as a narrow trail slowly appears before me, the pebbles glowing softly into the distance as if to guide me through the darkness.

52

I take a deep breath, my hands clenching into fists at my sides before I force myself to step forward.

I have had enough of this realm. Of the so-called gods that dwell here and their childish games.

And yet, here I am treading a path I have spent a lifetime avoiding; one I swore I would never step foot on again.

Knowing where this is leading me, I nearly turn back. If it were not for Hazel, I would ... But this *is* for her.

And for her, for *us*, I will brave the very depths of hell.

I have no choice but to face what, rather *who*, lies at the end of this path.

The Moirai.

The guardians of fate itself.

Some call them Fate, while still others refuse to refer to them as anything at all. It is an age-old fear among mortals that speaking their names will draw them to you. That it will disturb the three old crones as they weave the threads of fate between their fingers.

One pluck from them is all it takes to alter an entire existence.

Or so they think.

Everything is always a bit more complicated than the mortal stories care to admit.

Still, there is no creature more powerful that dwells in all of the Underworld. Even Hades himself must bow to them, for they are the ones who allow him to govern over the rest.

I scowl at the thought of coming face-to-face with them again.

Yet, I still push on.

The Fates, being guardians of souls themselves, are among the few creatures I cannot outright kill ... And one of the few who do not hide their hatred for me.

Few dare to cross them, and those who do, often do not live long to tell the tale. I, on the other hand, have spent my entire life crossing them. Each time I strike a deal with a mortal, delaying the inevitable for those foolish, or brave, enough to come to me, I have gone against them; twisting and tangling their carefully spun fates.

I have no doubt they will be less than pleased to see me.

As I continue down the narrow trail, my mind races with memories of the last time I encountered the Moirai. It was not a pleasant experience, to say the least. They demanded a price for their knowledge, one that I was not willing to pay.

But this time ... this time, I have no choice. I need answers, and they are the only ones here able to provide them.

The path quickly becomes a maze as it winds up a mountain, the pebbles growing brighter even as everything else grows darker. Offshoots begin to appear, leading off in various directions, the difference so subtle that any lesser-minded creature is likely to wander down one instead.

I send my own shadows ahead, searching out the way forward even as it tries to elude me. They do not wish for me to find them, but even they cannot stop me.

The weight of the Moirai's presence grows thick in the air, a foreboding aura that surrounds them like a heavy cloak, and I can feel sharp eyes watching my every step.

Some belong to those doomed to wander here, their curse for attempting to go against the Moirai. Others are creatures of the Fates themselves, their eyes and ears in the realms here and beyond.

As I draw closer to the summit, a tree, with barren branches twisting in every direction and an arched opening through its trunk, looms overhead. On the branches, just barely visible in the glow of the path, are perched three-eyed ravens, their heads cocked as they chatter to one another.

Their beady eyes glint in the dim light as they watch me move beneath the tree, doing my best to ignore their presence. It is impossible not to notice the way several of them take to the sky, disappearing into the inky blackness on their way to forewarn their mistresses of my approach.

Stepping out of the tree, the oppressing darkness finally breaks into the softer shadows of night, a sure sign that I am drawing close.

That, or they already know I am here and are hastening me into their presence.

My jaw hardens, as does my resolve, and I press onward toward the mountaintop. The path suddenly opens up onto a clearing where I find a simple dwelling that looks as if it has been cobbled together from the very rocks of the mountain. It teeters on the edge of a cliff as it overlooks the entirety of the Underworld, allowing the Fates an unhindered view into the lives of the gods that they manipulate with the weaving of their threads.

It is a far cry from the grandiose palaces of the gods, but it is perfect for the Moirai.

For all they truly crave is control.

My shadows swirl up around me as I approach the home, knowing the beings that lie within. The Moirai's power is not something to be taken lightly, and I feel a sense of unease as I consider the possibility of whatever it is they might demand of me.

But I have come too far to turn back now.

Moving closer, a crack slowly appears in the stone, widening to allow me entry.

My hands clench at my sides as I glance behind me at the raven-covered trees as they watch me before peering into the utter darkness of their lair. My own shadows do not even dare to enter without my direct order.

If it were not for Hazel, I would turn back. I would leave this cursed place and never again darken its doorstep, let alone cross its threshold.

But this is for her.

And for her, I would face a thousand evils for even the slightest hope of joy returned to her.

Taking a deep breath in, I exhale heavily before stepping into the dark crevice.

As soon as I have stepped inside, the crack seals behind me and the pitch-black darkness lifts as a blinding light fills the space instead.

My steps falter as I squint against the light, and it takes a few moments before I am able to see anything at all. When my vision finally clears, I am standing in the center of a circular room filled with thousands upon thousands of candles.

The walls are made of the same stone as the outside of the dwelling, but carved into intricate works of art that catch and hold the light as it dances across them.

Before me are two sets of stairs, one leading up and the other leading down into the depths of the mountain. Each staircase seems to disappear into its respective destination.

"Death," calls out a soft voice in my head, and my stomach twists at the sickeningly sweet beauty of it. "You have finally come."

I watch as a woman's bare foot comes into view on the stairs above, slowly descending to reveal the rest of her to me.

She is draped in a flowing white dress that appears to shift and swirl around her like a living thing, the hem dragging across the stone floor with each step. Her hair is a cascade of gold, tumbling all the way to her feet in soft waves.

Her beauty is terrible to behold, just as unnatural and contrived as the smile that she sends my way.

"Clotho," I say, her name falling bitterly from my lips even as I try to keep my tone neutral.

She descends the final step, gliding across the room to stand before me. Her power is palpable, thrumming in the air around her like a living thing. I can feel it reaching out to touch me, to test me, and I stand tall under the weight of it.

"Come," she beckons, her voice resounding in my mind as she gestures toward the stairs leading into the mountain's heart. "My sisters are waiting for us."

I have to stave off a shudder of repulsion as I watch her slowly turn to make her way down the second flight of stairs before following after her. As we descend, the candles lining the walls flicker and dance, casting eerie shadows across the stone. The air grows thicker, the weight of the Fates' presence almost suffocating.

Reaching the next floor, we step into another cavernous room cut out of the side of the cliffside, a gaping hole at the far end looking out over the Underworld and the sheer drop below.

At the very center of the space is a circular loom, carved from a single massive tree, its roots and branches twisted up in wild chaos to allow for the intricate weaving of thread. Sitting around it are two women, identical in every way to their sister except for the colors of their hair and the threads they hold in their hands.

Lachesis, with hair as dark as the night sky, holds a thread that glows with an otherworldly silver light. Atropos, with hair as pale as moonlight, twists a thread that pulses with a deep red hue.

"Death has finally come to call on us, sisters," Clotho announces, her voice seeming to come from everywhere and nowhere at once, her lips never once moving.

"As we knew he would," comes another voice, this one darker, but no less nauseating. A voice that can only belong to Atropos.

"You are looking well, Death," the third voice says, this one quieter than the others. Lachesis, perhaps the most tolerable of the lot, though her lips still tilt up in a sly smirk that makes my skin crawl.

"I have been better," I reply, my voice colder than I intended.

Her smirk widens, and I can see the amusement in her eyes at this. The three sisters share a look at this, relishing in my discomfort.

"Of course, you would not be here otherwise," Atropos says.

"We have been expecting you for a long while now," Lachesis adds as Clotho joins them at the loom. "How cruel it is that fate kept you from us for so long."

I grit my teeth together at this, struggling to keep my temper in check as my eyes move over the three women. I know they are trying to provoke me to rage, but I will not allow myself to do so.

Not yet.

"Tell us, what brings you to our humble abode?" Atropos asks, her voice dripping with false naivety.

"I require your help," I answer, swallowing my pride.

"Is that so," she says, her eyes gleaming with delight. "And what could you possibly need from us?"

"I need answers," I say, my jaw clenching as I try to keep my voice even. "Information that only you can provide."

The Fates share a look, their eyes glinting in amusement at my request. They know the power they currently hold over me, and they are savoring it.

Finally, Clotho speaks.

"We can provide you with the answers you seek," she says, her voice soft and eerily melodic, "but there will be a price to pay."

As there always is. Nothing comes free in this world, especially when it involves fate.

"Very well, name your price," I say darkly.

Atropos leans forward, her eyes gleaming.

"Not so fast. We have other business to discuss first, Death."

"Your business, to be exact," Clotho adds.

"I do not have time for—"

"Sit," all three voices demand in unison.

Reluctantly, I step forward to take a seat opposite them, my eyes never leaving the three sisters as they continue to work at the loom, their fingers moving in a blur as they weave.

They say nothing for a long moment, their smiles never slipping as they keep their eyes fixed on me. It would be less disturbing if they would simply scowl at me as I know they wish to.

Still, I do not allow them to intimidate me. As much as we might abhor one another, there is little they can do to me that I do not allow.

"I—"

"You will have your chance to speak," Clotho interrupts.

"We will listen to your every word, but first you must listen to ours," Lachesis says.

"We have been watching you, Death," Atropos begins, her fingers moving faster over the loom. "Watching as you have meddled in our affairs time and time again."

Inhaling deeply, I prepare myself for the very lecture I was expecting. A moment passes as the three continue to stare at me.

"Why is it that you cannot leave well enough alone?" Clotho snaps, her eyes flashing.

"Why is it that you choose to tangle the webs we have so carefully woven of mortal fate?" the middle sister adds.

I do not answer even as their eyes bore into me, daring me to defend myself. The silence stretches on, and

I can feel the weight of their gazes upon me. I grit my teeth, holding back the retort that threatens to spill from my lips.

"Speak!" Atropos hisses.

"I do what is necessary," I say, meeting their gaze unflinchingly. "You may deal in fate, but I deal in souls. I am the one who must carry out the ultimate reaping of the lives that you toy with. Why should I not have some say in what happens to them?"

The women's smiles all slip, just slightly, as they each cock their heads at me.

"Because," Clotho says, "it is our carefully woven threads that make sure all things work in accordance with the ultimate plan of the universe."

"It is our hands that make sure lives are spent according to their measure."

"Is that what you think?" I growl. "Is that what you tell yourselves when the innocent die too soon? When cruelty is allowed to run rampant? When murderers, abusers, and other such vile people outlive their victims?"

The Fates are silent, their expressions unreadable. The only sound in the room is the soft swishing of the loom as they continue to work, the threads of fate dancing between their fingers.

I can feel the tension in the air, and I know that I have struck a nerve, but I do not back down. I have come too far to be cowed by these three sisters who think they can control everything.

"It is the way of life," Lachesis whispers.

"No, it is *your* way."

"You are not the only one who feels the weight of

death," Atropos says, her voice low and measured. "We too must bear witness to the atrocities that occur in the mortal realm. However, we must remain impartial, for the greater good."

I scoff at her words.

I have never known the Fates to be anything *but* partial.

"The greater good? For whom? How can there be any good in allowing such suffering to continue?"

Clotho clicks her tongue at this, shaking her head. "You have spent so much time focused on death that you have forgotten what it takes to live."

My eyes narrow on her as I all but snarl, "Do explain."

The three sisters look at one another and then all rise from the table. Together they move to stand before the gaping hole in the cliffside, gazing out over the sprawling realm.

I watch as they stand there, the wind whipping through their hair as they survey the world below.

"Life is about balance," Clotho says, finally breaking the silence. "For every death, there is birth. For every ending, there is a new beginning. We may control the threads of fate, but it is the mortals themselves who weave the tapestry of life. They are the ones who give meaning to the lives they live."

"You may disagree with our choices, but you of all beings cannot deny that without death, life would lose much of its meaning," Atropos adds.

I hold my tongue, biting back the argument that rises within me at their words. The more they speak, the less I truly believe they care for the lives they thread.

"Regardless of what you may think, we do not control these mortals you care so much about," the middle sister says. "Yes, we do measure and intertwine their lives, but only according to the choices they make."

"And yet, you cut short the lives of many who do not deserve such a fate."

"Yes," the blonde answers sharply, "but you do not see the effect of our choices. You have been blinded to—"

"Been blinded?" I cut in, their choice of wording striking me as odd.

Their backs are still to me, though I sense their attention has now shifted to me, away from the city below.

The sisters hesitate, glancing at one another before Clotho continues, "You *are* blind to the consequences of the mortals' free will. What we do ensures the fate of the universe. We cannot stop cruelty from existing, only work to use it for the ultimate good of all."

"We must watch the threads, deciding when we must allow terrible things to happen," Lachesis says, "and when to simply cut a life short."

"But these deals you make with them interfere with our work, twisting fate and the very course of the universe," the white-haired sister hisses.

"You know I have little choice but to accept when a soul is offered to me in payment."

"Which is why you were ordered not to leave your realm," Atropos snaps. "You command the very shadows to do your bidding, and yet you cannot seem to leave well enough alone. No, you must find reasons to venture into the mortal realm. To play God over life and death, over the very course of history, with these deals you make."

My jaw clenches at this. I am finding it harder and harder not to speak out of turn.

"What is it then that you would have me do?" I ask, unable to keep the ice out of my voice.

The Fates share a look, a silent conversation passing between them, before turning back to look at me. Their smiles have returned, brighter than before as they take a step toward me.

And I know I have given them the opportunity they were looking for. I have tempted them with an open invitation to tell me exactly what it is they want from me.

"In exchange for what you want, we would like to propose something," Clotho says.

"An offer of our own, if you will," Lachesis adds.

"A deal with Death," they all chuckle darkly.

8

HAZEL

Finally dragging myself out of the bath, I quickly wrap a towel around myself and make my way over to the dress I laid out on the bed earlier.

Holding up the long lengths of silk, I frown as I turn it over in my hands. I do not know what to make of it, and try as I might to remember how Florence dressed me, I cannot figure out how to put it on properly.

Tossing it aside in exasperation, I turn back to the wardrobe and search through the other dresses. I'm just about to give up when my eye catches on a pile of fabric crumpled in the back corner.

Pulling it out, I smile as I hold it up before me.

Though it's the same deep midnight color as the other dresses, this one is made of a fabric so opaque it almost seems to absorb the light around it. Not to mention I can actually figure out how to wear it.

Quickly slipping it on, I return to the bathroom. The fabric is soft against my skin, sending shivers racing down my spine with each step I take.

Stopping before the mirror, I frown as I catch sight of myself in it.

The dress is far too loose, making me look more like a shapeless creature than a woman to be desired. This will not do.

Hurrying back to the bedroom, I snatch the lengths of silk from the bed and set about modifying the dress as best I can.

It's not long before the simple dress has been turned into something much more alluring ... and, having taken Eros' lessons into consideration, slightly less modest.

With the silk wrapped around my waist to cinch the fabric in, the sleeves have slipped off my shoulders, leaving my neckline more than a little exposed. But at least now I appear to have curves, and, thankfully, no matter how much I wriggle, the dress seems to be securely in place.

Pinning the long lengths of my hair away from my face, I watch as they spill down my back in unruly waves. Somehow, it seems to enhance the strange, almost beautiful chaos of my current ensemble.

As I stare at my reflection in the mirror, I can't help but feel a sense of power surging through me. I no longer look like the helpless, dirty girl from before; now, I look like a woman who knows what she wants ... and who will do whatever it takes to get it.

I just hope it will be enough.

With newfound confidence coursing through my veins, I make my way back to the bed to wait.

Settling onto it, I realize I need to come up with a more solid plan before Hades calls on me. I can't rely on just my appearance and charm to win him over, the other women have more than enough of both to drown me out a thousand times over.

I need to have a plan of action.

A way to truly convince him of who I am.

It seems strange that I must prove that I am who I say I am ... and the more I think about it, the less certain I become.

How does one prove themselves to someone who does not know them in the first place?

Of course, you cannot. Besides, I do not need to prove who I am, I only need to prove that I am the woman he wants.

I let out a small snort of disgust at this.

My fingers move over the dress and the simple modifications I've made. I hate how exposed I feel. This is not who I am or who I want to be.

It's one thing to pretend to seduce Hades, but another thing entirely to commit to doing just that.

I simply cannot allow things to go too far. Though even I know it would be impossible to stop him if it were to come to that, and I shudder just thinking about it.

I can feel my resolve already slipping through my fingers.

And then there's Persephone.

I can't stop myself from thinking about her, and my stomach twists with discomfort. Guilt and shame flood through me. I'd seen the pain on her face at the ball.

She is one of the few beings who has tried to help me, and this is how I plan on repaying her kindness?

I hate everything about my plan, but I don't know

what else to do. The more I try to come up with any other way to go about this, the less certain I am that there is another way.

Not now that I'm alone. If Death were here ... I shake my head, pushing the thought aside.

I cannot dwell on what I've done.

I must focus on the task at hand ... on surviving long enough to hopefully save the ones I love.

Still, the last thing I want is to come between Persephone and Hades. For goodness' sake, I'm not even interested in Hades, nor do I wish to break her heart.

Gods know I do not want to be the one responsible for that.

If only there was some way for me to get word to Persephone, to let her know of my plan. To assure her that I have no interest in her husband other than to save my father's life, if not my own.

Deep down, I believe she would understand.

Taking a deep breath, I curl up on the bed, my eyelids growing heavy from the churning of my mind.

As much as I dislike this plan, I have to remind myself what this is about. Who I am doing this for. At the very least, I have to *try* to save my father's soul.

I'll never be able to live with myself again if I don't.

My eyes drift shut before I can spiral any further, and at long last, sleep takes me.

I'm awakened by the sound of a key turning in the lock, my heart leaping into my throat as I suddenly sit up in bed. I turn to look just as a guard opens the door.

"You are to follow me to the dining hall for dinner," he says, barely glancing my way.

"Dinner?"

I blink in surprise, turning to look out the window only to see that the daylight has begun to fade. Quickly rising from the bed, I do my best to smooth out my skirt and hair before nodding to the man.

Quietly, he leads me out of the room and down the stairs of the tower. I chew my bottom lip, wanting to ask questions but knowing that he won't answer them.

Instead, I busy myself by taking in as much as I can as we make our way down the spiral staircase and through the sapphire palace.

The guard's pace is far too quick for me to catch more than a glimpse of the rooms and floors we pass. I suppose, for now, I'm to remain in the dark when it comes to finding my way about this place.

The longer we walk, and the nearer we possibly draw to Hades, the more nervous I become. My hands worry the smooth material of my dress, the hemline sweeping over the stone floor as our footsteps echo through the empty halls.

I can only hope I've done enough to catch his eye again.

When we finally reach the large dining room, the guard pulls the doors open to allow me to step inside, and I'm surprised to find the other women already seated within.

Of course, the guard chooses this unfortunate moment to suddenly announce my presence with the loud clearing of his throat. I freeze, my cheeks burning with embarrassment, as everyone turns to look our way.

"Move," the guard says, shoving me forward when my feet refuse to obey.

The man stops at an empty seat in the middle of the room. Not so gently pushing me toward it, I take my seat and the guard disappears.

An uncomfortable silence fills the room as we await Hades.

I nervously lift my eyes to peer around the dining hall, taking in the heavy velvet curtains at the windows and the intricate carvings and ornate tapestries that adorn the walls. Even the table has a dark silk runner, and the flickering candles are a deep, nearly black sapphire.

Yet again, I'm reminded of what I expected Death's home to be like. The cold chill of the place racing down my spine, despite the heat.

Despite the opulence, a feeling of dread settles in the pit of my stomach, growing more nauseating with each passing second.

It isn't long before the women begin to whisper amongst themselves, casting furtive glances in my direction.

I can't help but notice that they're all dressed in fine silks and jewels, their hair styled in intricate braids and curls. I feel out of place in my makeshift dress and simple hair.

I can feel their judgment and disdain, and it only adds to my anxiety.

Perhaps there was no need for me to worry about my plan after all. How am *I* supposed to draw his attention when I cannot even begin to compare to those around me?

Just when I'm not sure I can take this any longer, the doors are thrown open with a bang, and in strides Hades.

He's dressed in black pants and a midnight blue shirt that he's currently rolling up over his forearms as he makes his way through the hall, the squeak of his leather boots filling the silence that's fallen over the room. Despite the casual nature of his attire, there's a dangerous air about him that makes my blood run cold.

Although the room is already quiet, a deeper hush falls over us as we watch him move toward the head of the table. His head is held high, and his eyes don't waver from his destination.

When he finally takes his seat, the room seems to reach a tipping point.

"Welcome, ladies. I trust you have all been treated well in my absence," Hades says, and it's as if the whole room lets out a collective sigh as the silence is at long last broken. "Come, let us eat."

As if on cue, servants slip from the shadows to place silver plates laden with strange meats and vegetables before us. I stare down at the food, the smell of spices and herbs filling my nose as the other women begin to dig in.

I know that I need to eat to keep up my strength, but I'm hesitant to take a bite of anything on my plate. I'm not sure I could even swallow a bite if I wanted to, no matter how tempting it looks.

Quiet conversation fills the room along with the sounds of knives dragging against plates and cups being placed down on the table. My mouth waters as I watch them eat, yet my stomach is too tightly knotted for me to dare touch any of the food.

Still, I can at least pretend.

Picking at the food on my plate, I let my eyes wander around the room again, only now realizing that Persephone has yet to join us.

Where is she? Is it normal for her not to dine with him?

It seems odd that a wife, let alone a queen wouldn't take supper with her husband, and it leaves me feeling more than a little worried.

There goes any hope of letting her in on what I was planning to do.

Without meaning to, my eyes keep shifting back toward the head of the table, though I barely register what I'm doing ... until I refocus to realize Hades looking right back at me.

I start, nearly dropping the fork in my hand as I quickly pull my eyes away from him. The knots in my stomach tighten as I try my best to calm my racing heart, thankful that my stomach is too empty to allow me to be sick.

Slowly, I peek back up at him, only to find his narrowed gaze remains locked on me. His brow furrows as our eyes meet, and again I look away to feign interest in the mostly untouched food before me.

It's only as I start to push a brazed carrot around my plate that I realize I'm already failing my own plan. I'm supposed to be charming him, not hiding my face every time he happens to glance my way.

How else am I supposed to prove to him that I am the woman he's searching for, the one he danced with at the ball?

"Is the food not to your liking, mortal?" Hades asks coldly, just as I take a deep breath and lift my eyes to look his way again.

"Of course not," I say, my words catching in my throat, "I—"

"The mortals have always been an ungrateful lot, my lord," a golden-haired woman sitting to my left says. "It does not surprise me that she cannot tolerate food fit for the very king of the Underworld. Such a waste."

I glance at her, my thoughts momentarily pulled away from Hades and my plans to charm him, as she sneers at my untouched food. I blink as I look down at my own plate, guilt weighing on me yet again. She's not entirely wrong, it does seem like such a waste, especially considering how many nights I went to bed with only the pangs of hunger to occupy my thoughts and fuel my nightmares.

Still, I cannot allow this woman's comments to veer me off course. Giving her a polite smile, I turn my attention back to Hades, but he is no longer looking our way. Instead, he's turned his attention toward a dark-haired woman who's seated closer to him.

She's stunning, a true beauty with dark, flowing locks, and full curves that make my own body feel inadequate and plain. Looking at her, I can hardly blame him for losing interest in me so quickly.

I watch as she smiles up at him, her full lips spreading into a soft smile as she nods along to whatever it is that he's saying. He barely even glances at his plate or cup as he continues to dine.

She has captured his entire attention, and I'm suddenly unsure how to have it returned to me.

Sighing, I look down at my food again.

With a room full of women like her, what reason does Hades have to notice me, a mere mortal?

If things were different, I would be grateful that his attention has been diverted, but as much as I may want to let his gaze pass over me, I cannot allow that to happen.

If I am ever going to earn his favor, he has to notice me.

He has to recognize me as the woman from the ball.

A shudder works its way down my spine as I realize that I need even more than that from him ...

I need him to fall for me.

9

HAZEL

Before I can gather the courage to do something stupid enough to catch his attention, the sound of a chair scraping against the stone draws everyone's attention toward the head of the table.

Hades rises slowly, his gaze sweeping through the room as silence quickly falls over us.

"I suppose it is time I tell you exactly why you have been made ... guests here," the king says, his words almost seeming to hang in the air.

I frown, glancing about the room as most of the women breathlessly await his every word.

Did he not already tell us why we were here?

If I can just figure out a way to prove myself to him, then the others won't have to be kept prisoner here any longer.

"One of you, as I have already said, captured my attention last night," he continues, straightening as he begins to walk slowly around the long table, "and yet, she remains elusive, hidden from my sight once more."

His gaze lingers on me for a moment, and I feel a flicker of hope ignite in my chest until he turns his attention back to the dark-haired woman from before. My heart sinks as he continues his leisurely circle around the table, his eyes never once returning to me.

"And so, I have decided we will play a little game."

"A game?" one of the women whispers before quickly pressing a hand to her mouth.

"Yes, instead of trying to force this woman to reveal herself, I will give each of you the chance to prove yourselves to me. Do so wisely, for I intend to make the woman who earns my favor my next wife."

I blink in utter shock at this. The women around me gasp, many of them looking elated at the prospect, while still others look as horrified as I feel.

Wife? But what about Persephone?

Surely, I must have misheard him, but I know I did not as the others echo whispers of my own confusion.

Hades seems pleased by the reaction as he takes his seat at the head of the table again.

"He is not worth your time, mortal," a woman sitting across from me whispers.

I glance up at her, taking in her soft green eyes and copper hair. She gives me a small smile that eases the painful knotting of my stomach.

If I cannot draw Hade's attention with my looks, then perhaps I can glean some information from those around me. This woman looks far more pleasant to have a conversation with, compared to the others around me that seem to stare down their noses at me.

"What do you mean?" I ask her.

"You have been trying to draw his attention all night," the woman says. "It is not worth your time. Forgive me for saying so, but Hades has only ever cared for the most elusive of women. He would never consider a mortal an acceptable bride."

She shakes her head at this, and I frown at her.

"Even if she really is the one that he's searching for?"

"Perhaps, as his temporary whore," she says. "But as his queen? No. It would be best for you to lay low and play your cards right so that you can get out of this hellish place as quickly as you can."

I blink at her, worry taking a stranglehold on me once again as I glance toward the head table. Surely, she must be wrong, why else would he keep me here among the others?

"He would be fortunate if a mortal, no matter how inconsequential they may be, found him interesting enough to share a conversation with," I said.

The woman's eyes go wide as my words seem to carry through the room. I can almost feel everyone turning to glance at me, wondering who was foolish enough to mutter such a thing aloud. My cheeks burn with the sudden attention, but I'm unable to stop the next words to leave my mouth.

"In fact, it seems fortunate that any of us are willing to offer him our time when he's clearly blind to the beauty of his own wife. Perhaps he should focus on fixing his own marriage before trying to find a new queen."

"Hazel," the woman gasps as she drops her gaze into her own lap, and the room falls into a stunned silence at my words.

The very air seems to freeze around me, a chill spreading through me the moment I realize I've said too much. I don't even have to turn my head to know I've finally gained Hades' attention.

Though I can feel the weight of his gaze on me, I refuse to back down. This may be my only chance to prove myself to him. But as the room seems to darken with each passing second, I wonder if perhaps I've made a grave mistake.

The weighty silence filling the room is only disturbed when Hades shoves back his chair and it clatters to the floor as he rises to lean forward over the table.

"Leave us," he orders, his voice cold and menacing. "Everyone but the mortal, out."

Not a single word is spoken as everyone quickly rises and begins to file out. My heart beats rapidly in my chest as the chairs around me empty.

I keep my eyes trained on the plate before me as the doors to the room close, flinching slightly at the loud bang. Then I hear the drawn-out approach of Hades' footsteps as he moves toward me.

He comes to a stop behind my chair, the hairs on the back of my neck standing as he leans down, one hand coming to rest on my bare shoulder.

"You speak out of turn, mortal," he says.

"If my words have offended you," I say quickly, hoping to placate him in some way, "I only meant—"

"I know what you meant. Your lies mean nothing to me," he growls. "You would do well to learn your place in this realm, or you will suffer the consequences."

"I only—"

"Do you really think I am so blind to the world around me that I do not know who you are?" he hisses, cutting me off as his breath tickles the hairs on the back of my neck.

I blink at this, his words taking me by surprise. Is it possible he's finally recognized me as the woman from the ball?

"As alluring as Death may find you," Hades continues, "I will not be won over so easily. I know you are the little mortal who tried to weasel her way out of my kingdom."

"And, so what if I am?"

He pauses before saying, "Do not think I cannot see what you are doing."

"What is it that you think I am doing?"

"Exactly what you first came here for. You are trying to escape."

Another shiver runs down my spine at this, could I really have been such a fool to think he wouldn't see through my plan?

Still, I do my best not to let him see that his words have fazed me.

"If you despise mortals so, and I am not the woman you seek ... Then why keep me here? Why not allow me to leave?"

He chuckles softly at this.

"Because I can," he says, pressing his mouth closer to my ear as he trails the backs of his fingers down my neck. "Besides, who said anything about despising you? After all, you are still in the running to become my next wife."

With that, he finally straightens and he steps back from my chair.

I warily turn to watch as he turns and strides toward the doors leading out of the dining room, leaving me alone at the table.

I sit there for a moment, stunned by the turn of events. I had hoped to prove myself to him, to gain some sort of leverage in this dangerous game I'm playing. But now, I realize just how little power I truly have.

Hades pulls open the doors but pauses to glance back over his shoulder at me.

"Another thing, mortal," he says. "You are never to speak of my wife to me again."

"Why?" I ask before I can stop myself.

I don't expect him to answer, so I'm surprised when he remains standing still in the doorway, a flurry of emotions flickering across his face. Then a stone mask of emotion settles over his features as his next words pierce me to my core.

"Because she is as good as dead to me now."

He steps from the room before any more of my questions can bubble out, and I'm left staring at the cracked doors in stunned silence. I can just make out the silhouette of a guard before the doors open again, and I'm given no choice but to follow him as I rise from my chair.

My mind is a mess of thoughts as the guard leads me back through the empty halls and up the spiraling steps to my room in the tower. I barely even register the sound of the door closing before I hear the clicking of the lock.

In a daze, I move to sit on my bed.

A tiny flower of hope has begun to blossom in my chest. Perhaps there's even more to this story than I realized, and it's given me an idea.

One that, hopefully, won't involve me having to seduce him.

One that could solve things for everyone here ... but first I must find a way to speak with Persephone.

Or, at the very least, get word to her.

HADES

"Has Eris done as I have requested," I ask, not bothering to look at Deimos as I throw open the doors to the room.

"She has, my king."

"And Persephone?"

"She will do exactly as she has been told," Deimos says.

"Good, then everything is going to plan."

"Yes, my king."

"Make sure that she does not get time alone with any of the women, particularly the mortal."

Deimos bows his head in acknowledgement of my order. "Is there anything else you require?"

I pause, resting a hand on the back of a chair as I consider his question for a moment.

"Yes, actually," I say, turning my gaze to Deimos. "I want you to personally keep an eye on Persephone. Eris may have done as I asked, but I do not trust her."

"As you wish, my king."

"Good. Then that will be all for now," I say, dismissing him with a wave of my hand.

"Of course."

Once he has left the room, I take a deep breath as I chuckle to myself.

The plan is in motion, and I can almost taste the power surging through me as I think of what is to come.

The mortal will be mine, and with her by my side, I will be unstoppable.

I stride over to the window and look out over the kingdom, my eyes scanning the horizon.

"Soon, we shall learn if a kingdom can truly be borne of a mere mortal."

11

EROS

I let out an exasperated sigh, crossing my arms over my chest, as I stand before the gates to the Underworld once again.

It took longer than I expected to get through the forest, and I am not sure how many hours I lost among the trees. Though, judging by the fading light, it was far too many.

Of course, Death is nowhere to be found now, not that I expected him to just be standing around where Hazel left him ... though, I suppose a small part of me did, but there is no trace of him.

Stepping closer to the gate, I reach out to make sure the mortal's father is still held firmly to the gate when a hand grabs my wrist from the other side.

"What are you doing?"

"Who are *you* to question me, mortal?" I scoff, pulling my hand back as strength is pulled from me at his touch.

"Did you hurt her? Is she here?"

"What are you talking about?"

"Hazel, is she here? Is ... is that what happened to her?"

I freeze, a chill racing over my skin as I take a step back, my unseeing eyes shifting about as if trying to put a face to the voice.

"Who asks?"

"Her brother."

I frown at this, trying to recall if I ever heard her mention a brother ... and if so, what she told me of him. But I simply cannot remember.

"Wait, what are *you* doing here?"

"You have yet to answer my questions," the young man says coolly.

I narrow my gaze at him, knowing full well how unsettling I can appear to mortals as I draw myself up.

"As I said before, I owe you no explanation. You are in *my* realm now, and you would do well to remember it."

"You—"

The young man is cut off by a sudden cry, and the next thing I know, he has disappeared into the thick of the ever-growing sea of souls.

A curse escapes me as I shift out of my human form and lift my snout to the air. Even in my animal form, I cannot scent him. I do not even know his name to draw him toward me. There are too many souls wandering on the other side for me to make heads or tails of anything.

What the hell is going on around here?

I have to find Death, and quickly.

But at this rate, I will have to set off in a random direction and hope luck is on my side. Before I can act on my frustration though, I am startled by a low growl; the hairs on the back of my neck standing on end as I slowly turn.

Cerberus, I wrinkle my nose at the smoky scent of him, frustrated with myself for not having noticed his presence before. The giant hellhound approaches slowly, obviously less than thrilled to find his gates have collected a god.

"What are you doing here?" he asks, making a sound of disgust as we both shift into our human forms.

"Well, hello to you as well," I say, plastering a smile onto my face.

"Why are you standing before my gates, Eros?" Cerberus asks again, his voice low and threatening. "It is unlike you to leave the pleasures of your own home for that of the mortal world."

The way he spits out *pleasures* has my smile wavering. I am no stranger to what others think of me and what I stand for.

And yet, given the chance, all of them would climb into my bed if I were to so much as suggest it.

I am accustomed to ignoring the looks that are sent my way when I leave the walls of my palace behind, as if they are not guilty of indulging in the same pleasures themselves ... and often behind the backs of their own wives and husbands.

As if *I* am to blame for their unfaithfulness.

"I am flattered that you know anything about me," I say. "I cannot imagine you have much free time to know much of anything when all you do is prance about as Hades' loyal lapdog."

"I know enough."

I snort at this.

"Still, I am impressed you have the capacity in that little head of yours to have a single thought of your own."

"I know more about the Underworld and its inhabitants than you could ever dream," Cerberus growls.

"Is that so?"

"Yes. For instance, I know that it must be something vitally important to have dragged all the way out here, alone."

I scoff at this.

"You could say that about anything."

"So, it would not be an issue to delay whatever it is you are trying to accomplish by hauling you back to the palace?"

My jaw hardens at this before I finally let out a deep sigh.

"Fine. If you must know, I am searching for Death."

Cerberus lets out an exasperated sound at this.

"He is still here then?"

"Yes. Now, if you will excuse me, it is important that I find him before it is too late."

"Be my guest."

Cerberus steps out of my path, surely just as eager to have me gone as I am to leave this horrid spot. I do not know how he is able to stomach watching the souls stumble as they do little more than mutter nonsense while awaiting their inevitable fates.

It is only as I think this that I realize this will be the girl's fate too, if we cannot find a way to save her.

I quickly move past Cerberus but stop a few steps ahead, turning back to face him.

"Will the gates be opened now that you are back?"

I can sense his suspicion before he even opens his mouth.

"Why?"

"To let all those souls in before they overwhelm this place with all their babbling," I say, waving a hand vaguely in the direction of the gates.

He laughs.

"Not that you actually care about what happens to them ... but no, they will not."

"Why not?"

"Why the sudden interest?" he retorts.

I let out a sigh before answering, "Perhaps I am simply taking an interest in things outside my own pleasure for once. Humor me, Cerberus, so I can be gone from here quickly."

"Because winter is coming," he answers. "The gates will not open again until Hades departs, and only for a day. They will not open again until his return in the spring. I should think you would know this by now, it is rather common knowledge among the court since ... At least, it has been for a while now."

"Right, of course. It must have slipped my mind."

Cerberus clearly does not believe me, but he says nothing to encourage the conversation to continue.

Giving him a nod, I turn and once again move away from the gates. As I walk, I cannot help but wonder why Persephone did not mention this little fact.

Perhaps it is common knowledge, but I do not recall hearing of this change. Moreover, it seems like something

Persephone should have made sure Death and Hazel were aware of.

If nothing else, we might have been able to plan things out a little differently ...

Though, the more I think about it, the less I am sure it would have made any difference.

"Eros," Cerberus calls out.

Groaning, I turn back to face the insufferable man.

"What is it now, Cerberus?"

"You are going the wrong way."

"And how do you know that?"

"I am a *dog*, after all, Eros. Surely you do not need to ask such useless questions."

My annoyance flares as I picture every single way tiny misfortune may befall this irksome creature. The very smugness of his attitude does little to make me want to listen to what he says. Yet, I force myself to wait.

Without a word, he turns and begins to stride off in another direction, his footsteps pausing after a moment as he calls out over his shoulder, "Well, are you coming or not?"

I frown, unsure of whether or not to follow him.

"Why do you want to help me find Death?"

"I have unfinished business with him. So, either you can follow me. Or—and I admit I *am* hoping you choose this option—you can let me drag you back to the palace and let Hades question you first. The choice is yours."

I let out a frustrated sigh.

"Fine, just hurry up and lead the way."

Cerberus turns so his back is to me as he continues,

his hellhound senses picking up on something I cannot seem to find.

I stay where I am for a moment longer, the very thought of having to spend another second in this man's presence annoying me more than it should.

But it appears that I do not really have a choice.

Doing my best to swallow my irritation, I hasten to follow after Cerberus.

To find Death, and to rescue the mortal's soul.

Hopefully, before it is too late.

12

HAZEL

In my absence, someone must have been sent up to my room as there is now a simple nightgown laying out on the bed. I quickly check the rest of the room, but there is no one else here with me.

I pace back and forth for a while in thought before eventually changing and slipping beneath the silk covers of the bed. Sleep evades me as I try to come up with some way of getting word to Persephone, but the more I think, the more impossible it seems.

The guards are already unwilling to glance my way, let alone speak to me ... I don't even have any paper to write a note on.

My mind stills at this, suddenly remembering the package I'd found on Death that I'd managed to tuck into my skirt earlier.

Praying that it survived everything that's happened since last night, I throw off the covers and scramble out of bed. As I hurry toward the bathroom, the door to the bedroom is thrown open with a startling bang.

91

I spin around, stumbling back against the nearest wall as two guards walk into the room.

"What is the meaning of this?" I demand, wrapping my arms around myself. Of course, they remain silent as they step forward to grab me.

My heart pounds as I do my best to struggle against their iron grips, but I'm unable to get away from them as they grab my arms. The men drag me from the room and down the stairs, my bare feet barely able to keep up as they slip over the dark stone. I can't even make sense of where they're taking me thanks to the dim light of the hallways.

Terrified, we finally stop before a set of large doors made of dark wood that almost seem to swallow me up as they open. The guards shove me inside, and I stumble forward into a cavernous, softly-lit room.

Straightening, I find myself greeted by the blinking faces of the other women Hades has taken prisoner, each one looking just as lost and confused as I feel.

Before I can turn to try to question the guards, they've already retreated, the doors pulled tightly shut behind them.

Thankfully, the women quickly lose interest in me, and I am left to explore the room on my own.

It's cavernous, most of it still shrouded in shadows, and overgrown with wild vines and flowers. It's as if a small indoor jungle has simply sprung to life within Hades' walls.

My steps carry me toward the back of the room where I discover an elegant set of chairs and a lounge, and hope rises in my chest as I pray this room belongs to the goddess that I think it does.

But, as time ticks by, I grow more nervous and uncertain that it does.

"Hazel?"

I glance up to find the red-haired woman who spoke to me at dinner approaching me tentatively.

"How do you know my name?" I ask, inwardly kicking myself for not thinking to seek her out earlier.

Her eyes fill with worry as she glances around the room before drawing closer.

"My name is Lilia, I am of Eros' court," she answers.

"Oh," I gasp, "do you have any news from outside? From Eros?"

She shakes her head.

"No, I am afraid not. I was taken from my home and husband early this morning, and we have not been allowed communication with anyone beyond these walls."

Of course, I should have guessed as much.

I chew my lip, feeling a pang of guilt at the thought of having dragged all these innocent women into this mess. They don't deserve to be caught up in Hades' twisted games.

"I'm sorry," I say, my voice barely above a whisper. "I didn't mean to get you all involved in—"

"Nonsense," Lilia interrupts. "This is Hades' doing, not yours. I ... I only wish to advise you not to give up on love so quickly, and certainly not in favor of the king."

"Excuse me," I say, blinking at her in surprise.

"Forgive my forwardness, but my husband tends to the gardens and last night—"

Suddenly, darkness sweeps through the room. Several women cry out in fear, drowning out Lilia's voice, as they all step closer to one another.

A strange heaviness falls over the room as a soft glow fills the space around us before pooling in the center of the room. Slowly, a figure materializes before the light rushes out to fill the room again, revealing Persephone in a burst of soft petals.

Uneasy relief washes over me as I watch her gaze sweep over the room.

I force myself to remain rooted to the spot, despite my urge to rush toward her and tell her everything. Something doesn't feel quite right, and I need to see what happens next before I reveal myself to Persephone.

So, I wait and watch as she takes several steps forward.

As Persephone moves away from the center of the room, flowers bloom in the wake of her footsteps. But the further she moves away from them, the quicker they wither away back into nothingness.

Vines snake up around her bare legs, twisting about her calves without hindering a single step as she glances about the room. Though her lips are pulled into a smile, it does little to hide the sharpness lurking within her eyes.

There's an anger ... a bitterness to her that I haven't seen before.

I take a step back just as Lilia shifts slightly to get a better view of Persephone; and although I can still just make her out around the tall woman, I'm momentarily hidden from the goddess' view.

I do my best to calm my thudding heart as I wait for her to speak. To let us know why we've been brought here in the middle of the night.

Persephone stops a few feet away from the other women, the strange light spilling over her giving her an eerie but not quite ethereal glow.

The vines and flowers continue to burst to life at her feet, wrapping around her legs and clothing her in foliage nearly halfway up her torso. Still, it's strange to watch as the flowers die nearly as quickly as they bloom, only to immediately be replaced by a new bud.

I don't recall seeing this happen the last time I saw her. Nor do I recall her seeming so out of control with her emotions.

She's definitely not acting like any version of herself that I know.

The tension in the room grows, curiosity mixing with anxious anticipation as the women begin to shift uncomfortably on their feet.

Still, Persephone remains silent as her eyes slowly move over the room yet again.

"I know what Hades' intentions are with you," she says, finally breaking the uneasy quiet even as her words weigh heavily in the air. "And I know that one among you has already caught his eye. I not your queen?! Would you betray my kindness to become my husband's second wife?"

Her voice rings through the room, causing everyone

to flinch. Persephone holds up a hand as she takes a deep breath to calm herself.

"And yet, as is the way of my husband, I have no say in the matter. So, I have decided to help prepare you for your future role."

Shock hits me as I try to make sense of what I just heard.

Why would she even agree to help her husband find a new lover? Wouldn't that put her own place at court, her very life, in danger?

This makes no sense to me. Surely, she cannot mean what she says.

Or, perhaps like us, she has no choice.

"Now, I will tell you why I have gathered you all here. Every day that you remain in this palace, after my husband has retired for the night, you will be brought here to me," she says, slowly pacing in front of us. "And every night, I will instruct you in what it takes to please Hades. After which, one of you will be sent up to him."

This causes an outburst of whispers from the woman, my own heart pounding at the implication of her words. The fury in her eyes intensifies as she allows the murmuring to continue for a moment before summoning silence with the lifting of a hand

Nodding once as silence is granted, she continues, "Should the chosen woman successfully win over my husband, the rest of you will all be allowed to leave and return to your lives."

Persephone pauses as several of the women let out relieved sighs at this, but I'm unwilling to let my guard down just yet.

"However, if the woman is unsuccessful in her attempts, she will not return to see another day. This cycle will continue until one of you manages to win him over, or none of you remain."

A deadly silence falls over the room, and Persephone's expression grows harder as she looks over the women once more. Again, this version of the beautiful spring goddess seems so unlike the woman I met only days ago.

I can feel the terror wafting off the women trapped here with me. I don't know how much longer I'll be able to bear this feeling of guilt, especially now that these women's lives are at stake. Women who are only stuck here because of me.

An icy shiver runs down my spine as I realize the true gravity of the situation that we have now found ourselves in.

This is no game.

This is a challenge.

This is a fight for our very survival.

"We begin tonight," Persephone announces, drawing my focus sharply back to her. Her gaze sweeps past me once before snapping back, suddenly noticing me despite Lilia partially blocking me from view. Her eyes turn dark for a moment before warming into soft honey-green pools.

The change is so quick, I take a startled step back.

"Hazel?" she says, confusion flickering across her face for a second before she can shake it. "Come, stand by me."

Reluctantly, I force my feet to carry me toward her as

the other women eye me warily. She gives me a soft smile as she watches me, though her gaze sharpens again as I draw nearer.

I don't trust this version of Persephone, and I'm careful to stand as far from her as possible. I still can't shake the feeling that something more is at play here, but I do not yet know what.

"Persephone, I—"

"I will speak with you later," she says, turning back to face the others. "You will need to know everything there is to know about my husband and his ... desires. From this moment forward your likes, your desires, your very hopes and dreams are to become his."

Many of the women exchange uncertain looks at this as they continue to shift uncomfortably on their feet, but several seem all too eager to learn more. I force myself to remain still, trying my best to keep my face neutral and my emotions in check.

"We will begin with your demeanor," Persephone says, her voice taking on a sultry tone. "Hades is a powerful man, and he enjoys being in control. You must learn to be submissive, to let him take the lead, but do not mistake submission for weakness. You must be confident in your perceived innocence, make him believe you are worth his time and attention."

I frown at this, my confusion only growing the more she speaks, and it appears that she's genuinely trying to teach us how to seduce her husband.

The others seem to shift closer, suddenly curious about this lesson on how to please Hades. My frown deepens until Persephone glances at me. She smiles, and her teeth almost appear to flash and sharpen into points in the eerie glow.

"Here, I will use Hazel as an example," the goddess says, snapping my attention back to her as she steps closer.

Our eyes meet and I see nothing good buried in them. There is no kindness like I saw the day I met her.

I can't help but wonder if she knows this is all my fault, and if she does, what she intends to happen to me.

"Persephone," I start again, only to quickly my lips together when she gives me a warning look and continues her lesson.

"Follow my lead, and try to pretend that this girl is Hazel."

She approaches me, her movements fluid and graceful, and strangely disarming. I can feel the heat of her body as she comes near, the fresh scent of spring enveloping me. It's intoxicating, but I know better than to let my guard down.

She reaches up to brush a strand of hair behind my ear, and I fight the urge to flinch away from her touch.

"Now, observe how I touch her," she says, her voice low and dangerous. "You must learn to be sensual, to make him crave your touch ... without allowing him to think *you* want to bed him."

My muscles tense as she suddenly bends to pick something up and pretends to accidentally brush her body against me. Though her movements do little more than add to my discomfort, I have no doubt if I were a man, it would be quite a different story.

As she straightens, she gives the other women a

knowing look but continues to act as though she is innocent of her own actions.

"Hades is a man of particular tastes; he must always *believe* he is in charge," she says, her face softening as she drops her chin to look coyly up at me. "Make him believe he is the one hunting you, instead of the other way around."

One of the women lets out a snort of contempt at this, and Persephone immediately looks up just as the blonde from earlier finishes rolling her eyes.

I shudder as Persephone steps away from me, the softness immediately leaving her features as she narrows her eyes on the other women.

"Now it is your turn," she tells them. "Pair up and try your best to act out innocent allure on one another. Do not forget that the well-timed accidental slip of a dress sleeve or lifting of a hem can go further than you might think."

As the others pair up and I'm left standing awkwardly alone, it's a small relief to be momentarily forgotten by Persephone. I watch as she moves through the women, quickly correcting their actions and offering them words of advice. As the night wears on, I can't help but notice that I am the only one not actually participating.

Even if it hardly seems like much of a lesson at all ... but perhaps that shows just how little I know.

I wonder if she learned any of this from Eros, it seems just like the type of thing he would have taught me if we'd had longer to prepare. I have to bite back a laugh at this thought. No, I don't think he would have taught me anything quite so subtle.

Eros may be the God of Lust and Desire, but I get the sense he doesn't know what it takes to have to *earn* desire.

"That will be all for tonight," Persephone finally announces, returning to stand by my side without so much as a glance in my direction.

I might as well be a statue within this garden given how little attention she's paid me, but hopefully, that will change once we have a moment to speak alone.

Her eyes instead shift over the room as the women return to stand before her, and it hits me that she's choosing the first woman to send up to Hades' chambers. My stomach twists with discomfort as her eyes land on the rude, albeit beautiful, blonde who was sat next to me at dinner.

The smile that stretches Persephone's lips is nothing short of terrifying as she points to her.

"You," she says. "You will be the first to go to my husband. Your success or failure in this will decide the fate of not just yourself, but all those who stand in this room."

The blonde pales at the unspoken reminder that if she fails, she'll likely be dead by morning. I watch as those around her pull back slightly as if already preparing for her loss.

"Now?" the woman asks. "It is but a few short hours until dawn, and I—"

"Have you heard *nothing* that I have said?" Persephone snaps, cutting her off. "You will go to him this night and prove once and for whether or not you have what it takes to seduce the king."

The blonde straightens at this challenge, her own

face hardening as a cold smirk pulls at the corner of her mouth.

"Very well, *Your Highness.*"

"Guards!"

"Persephone," I whisper urgently, "please, may I speak with you."

"Not now," she answers just as a number of her guard step into the room. "Escort the others back to their rooms at once."

I watch in dismay as Persephone crosses to lounge on a chair at the back of the room before I'm herded out of the room with the other women.

It isn't until I'm back in the tower, the door closed and locked behind me, that I let out a sigh of both relief and frustration.

When the spring goddess first noticed me, I'd half expected to be thrown to Hades immediately. In some ways that would have been better.

Now that I'm stuck here, I can't help but wonder why I wasn't, and why Persephone hadn't allowed me a moment to speak with her.

Slipping into bed, I toss and turn but sleep evades me as I wait to learn of the woman's fate, to learn of all of our fates.

I worry that too many women will be lost to this game Persephone seems to be playing. No matter how I turn it over in my head, I just can't see what she hopes to gain from this.

Let alone what I'm supposed to do now.

13

HAZEL

Morning finds me sleep-deprived as I sit on the bed, knees pulled to my chest, staring out the single window of my room.

The second that the dark sky outside begins to lighten, I rise and cross over to the window. Pushing it open, I lean out to peer down at the still-slumbering realm below.

I'm given no hint as to whether the blonde was successful or not. Though, I'm not sure what I expected to find either way.

My heart beats steadily in my chest as I prepare for the worst.

Even now, I'm struggling to bring myself to accept that the Persephone I met before was nothing more than an illusion. Perhaps this ... this cold, cruel version of the goddess is her truest form.

And I fear that the absence of the woman she sent to him will only confirm how terrible things really are. That

I am nothing more than a foolish mortal trying to outplay the gods.

I shudder at the thought, yet again feeling Death's absence

Closing the window, I turn to dress for the day, my mind racing with thoughts of what's to come.

Throwing open the wardrobe with a sigh, I'm surprised to find a single dress hanging inside. Though it's made of the same midnight silk, it's simple and easy enough for me to slip on without help.

The bodice of the dress clings to my body, the silk draping in soft folds around my neckline, while the skirt flows softly to the floor, a thigh-high slit up one side.

I make my way into the bathroom to finish tidying up only to notice the stained gown I'd tossed in the corner the day before.

Hurrying over to it, a wave of relief washes over me as I feel a small bundle tucked within. Unwrapping the fabric, I pull out the brown package and clutch it tightly to my chest.

Almost in the same instant, I hear the sound of a key scraping in the lock. Slipping the package back into the folds of the fabric, I tuck it behind a small stool and emerge from the bathroom just as the door swings open.

He doesn't say anything as he motions toward the door, and for once I'm relieved the guards have no interest in speaking to me. Until I realize he's escorting me back to the dining hall.

My stomach twists with worry that this can only mean one thing, the woman was unsuccessful in her attempts to entice Hades.

Nervously, I step into the room. My eyes scan the somber faces already seated around the table, but just as I feared the woman from last night is nowhere to be seen. My shoulders sag in disappointment as I'm directed toward my seat.

Only, I'm not shown to the seat I had the night before, but the now empty one beside it. I try to protest, but the guard only roughly forces me down into the chair.

I feel the eyes of the other women on me, but they remain quiet as food is brought out to us. Glancing toward the head of the table, I cannot help but Hades' seat is empty.

"You should eat," Lilia whispers, drawing my gaze to her.

"You will not speak!"

She gives me a half-smile before returning to her meal, and I try to push myself to do the same. Lilia isn't wrong either, I do need to eat, despite my stomach wishing otherwise.

Taking a small bite, I'm pleasantly surprised to find my appetite suddenly returned. The rest of breakfast is a silent affair, with only the sounds of silverware scraping against plates to fill the room. No one so much as dares to cough, let alone say anything about the empty seat beside me.

As I finish a bit of cheese, I can't help the way my mind overflows with questions as I dare a glance about the table. Finally, the servants re-emerge from the shadows to clear our plates as the guards filter in behind our chairs.

Standing, I prepare myself for another long day spent

alone in my tower as my escort signals for me to follow him. With a small sigh, I step into place behind him as the other women walk ahead of us.

I watch them as we walk, wondering how many more of them will be lost before I can find a way to fix this. If there even is a way to fix this.

It takes me longer than I'd like to admit to realize that I'm not being taken back to the tower as we follow the other women through a series of wider and wider halls and down a short flight of stairs.

They look just as lost as I do as several of them glance back at me, as if double checking to see if we're all being brought to the same place. Silence follows us as I begin to fear we're in for another lesson from Persephone.

But we're not led to the jungle room we found ourselves in last night. Two of the guards in front push open a massive set of doors, steam wafting out in a heavy cloud to reveal a stunning bathhouse beyond. Pearly white tiles surround a pool of deep blue water that's unlike anything I've yet seen in Hades' palace.

I hesitate as I cross the threshold, my eyes widening in awe as I realize that this is more than just a simple bathhouse. This is a luxurious oasis in the midst of the iciness of the palace, complete with marble pillars and the sound of trickling water echoing off the walls.

"Welcome," a voice says from behind us, and I turn to find a beautiful, but rather unsettling woman standing behind us. She seems familiar, but I can't quite figure out why that is. She watches us all for a long moment, waiting to make sure she has everyone's attention before continuing, "You are to spend the day enjoying yourselves to the fullest here. Attendants have been provided to see to your every desire."

As if on cue, a line of gorgeous men appears behind her. Some carry towels and jars of oil, while still others are laden with platters of fruit and pitchers of wine, ready to pamper us in every possible way.

I follow the other women as they begin to undress, their garments falling to the floor in a pile of fabric as they wade into the water. Their eyes widen in pleasure as they sink into the steaming water.

Smiles and laughter are quick to replace the somberness that haunted us before. As if they've already forgotten that our very lives now hang in the balance.

I wish I could bring myself to relax, but I can't shake the feeling that something isn't right.

Wrapping my arms around myself, I look around the room, unsure of whether or not I should join them. Still fully clothed, I finally decide to sit at the edge of the pool.

I dip one foot in, smiling faintly at the soothing warmth of the water as it laps against my skin. The others begin to chat, their voices gradually growing louder as they aren't hushed or scolded into silence.

Movement catches my attention out of the corner of my eye, and I turn to look just as a handsome half-dressed attendant crouches down beside me.

"Is there anything I can do for you?" he asks, his eyes like molten amber beneath thick lashes.

For a moment, I hesitate before shaking my head.

"No, thank you. I am quite content as I am," I answer, dragging my eyes away from him and back to the glistening water.

He doesn't leave my side, though. In fact, he shifts closer. Nearly invading my space now, I have no choice but to glance at him.

"Are you sure there is *nothing* I can do to please you?" he presses, his honied eyes growing darker as he arches a brow.

It takes a second for the meaning behind his words to hit me, and I blink at him in stunned silence before a nervous laugh bubbles out of me. As beautiful as this man may be, there is nothing he could offer me that would tempt me away from this spot.

"Again, thank you, but no."

He frowns slightly at this but otherwise doesn't seem to care that I've now turned him down twice.

Much to my chagrin, he settles next to me instead. Dipping his own feet into the water, he shifts so that his thigh presses against mine.

"Come now, surely there is something I can do to bring you pleasure," the attendant whispers, his voice as low and soft as it is enticing. "I am quite talented in a number of ways."

I pull my leg away from his, a shiver running down my spine at his words. There is something unsettling about this place, and this man's persistence is not helping to ease my nerves.

"Be that as it may, I said no," I repeat firmly, my voice carrying a hint of warning.

I try to ignore the attendant's presence, looking away from him and focusing on the other women in the pool. But his words linger in my mind, and I find myself growing more and more uncomfortable by the second.

Still, he doesn't seem to take the hint. Instead, he reaches out and places a hand on my knee, his fingers trailing up my thigh through the slit in the dress.

I freeze, unsure of how to react. My instincts scream at me to push him away, to run as far from this man and this place as possible, but something keeps me rooted to the spot.

"Perhaps a massage then? I have been told that my hands are quite skilled," he suggests, his hand inching even higher up my thigh, "and there is nothing I will not do to please you."

"You can please me right now by removing your hand from my body," I hiss, my patience wearing thin.

He looks offended, his expression twisting into a scowl as he withdraws his hand. But before he can say anything else, a commotion at the other end of the pool draws our attention.

Turning, I find one of the other women in a rather delicate position with her own attendant. She lets out a moan, and I quickly drop my gaze as I realize what they're doing.

All at once, it's like a floodgate has been opened as others join her in seeking pleasure with their own attendants.

My cheeks flush, heat surging through my body, as I struggle to know what to do with myself when all I want is to run away. After my time spent in Eros' palace, you would think I'd be used to seeing this kind of behavior from the gods and creatures here, but I am not.

The man next to me leans in again, drawing my attention sharply back to him.

"Let us join them. I can show you things—"

I recoil, my heart pounding in my chest as I scramble to my feet, shaking my head at him. Words fail me as I stumble backward, unwilling to take my eyes off him lest he try to follow me, and slam straight into a wall.

Only, it isn't a wall.

Strong hands wrap around my arms, bracing me against a solid expanse of muscle before I can tumble to the floor.

Slowly I look up, expecting to find myself in the arms of another attendant, only to find something much worse.

Someone much worse.

Staring down at me, his expression unreadable even as blue flames flicker to life across his skin and hair, is Hades.

I gasp and hurry to put as much distance as possible between us, but he stops my retreat with a single, heavy hand on my shoulder. His grip is tight, unyielding, and I can feel the heat of his body pressed against mine, even as his eyes lift to take in the scene around us.

"Deal with them," Hades growls after a long moment, waving a hand at the women that have lost themselves to the pleasure of their partners.

Guards emerge from behind him, their armor glinting with refracted light from the water as they pour in to surround the pool. They move with practiced efficiency, separating the attendants from their clients and ushering them away without a word.

I watch in horror as many of the women are dragged out of the room in protest, crying out for mercy as they do their best to cover their naked bodies.

Nervously, I peek up at Hades.

A dark aura emanates from him like a suffocating cloud, twisting my stomach sickeningly. I thought he was the one who ordered us to be brought here, but from the way his eyes burn as he takes in the remaining women now cowering in the water, I am starting to think not.

Perhaps this was Persephone's doing then, but why?

"Take the rest back to their rooms," Hades orders, his fingertips digging into me.

I watch as the other women gather their things and are escorted from the room, thankful to see that Lilia is still among them as she sends a furtive look my way. As they pass, I suddenly realize that I should leave with them, but Hades' grip holds me firmly in place.

Glancing up at him, he doesn't meet my eyes.

"Not you."

My heart pounds in my chest as I try to swallow back my panic at his words. It isn't until the last of the guards and women are gone from the bathhouse that he finally loosens his grip on my shoulder.

Hades' hand drops to his side, and I step back, putting as much distance between us as I can without angering him. I can feel his eyes on me, burning into my skin, and I shiver involuntarily.

"How did you do it?"

I blink in confusion at his question.

"I-I'm afraid I don't understand," I stammer, my voice barely above a whisper. "How did I do what?"

Hades steps closer, quiet rage rolling off of him in heavy waves, as he reaches out to tilt my chin up, forcing me to meet his gaze.

111

"Rhyzihr, the incubus that was sent to seduce you. How did you, a mere mortal, resist him, when so many of my own court could not?"

I stare back at him in shock, not knowing what to say. Was it Hades, after all, who sent these men to tempt us? Was this one of *his* tests?

"Answer me!"

"I-I do not know him, let alone love him to allow such a thing to happen," I say.

Hades' raises a single brow at this as he continues to stare down at me. Curiosity flickers through his otherwise unreadable expression before he lets out a low snort.

"Love," he says, the word dripping from his lips like poison, "as if love were powerful enough."

Dropping his hand from my chin with a look of disgust, he dismisses me with a flick of his wrist. I don't hesitate to stumble away from him, even as one of Hades' men immediately appears at my side.

I cannot wait to be gone from this place, but I stop as I reach the door. Reminding myself that I'm supposed to be showing interest in him, I glance back over my shoulder.

Hades is watching me, his eyes burning with the same fire that I saw in him at the ball.

My heart lurches in my chest and I quickly turn away, suddenly not so sure that this is a game I want to be playing.

Least of all with Hades.

14

DEATH

The path leading away from the Fates' mountaintop dwelling is far less threatening in its eagerness for me to be gone.

Though the ravens still watch, moving from branch to branch as they chatter about my progress, I pay them no mind as I mull over everything that was said.

The sisters' words still echo in my ears, and I cannot help wonder but wonder if I made the right choice ... but only Hazel can be the judge of that now.

Sighing deeply, I stop to pull off my mask and run a hand over my face. The heat and cruelty of this realm presses down on me, and I cannot help but wish for this all to be over soon.

And yet, I would endure it a thousand times over if it only meant saving her.

Continuing on down the path, my heart is heavy as I come to terms with what that may entail. So lost in thought am I that I belatedly realize I am no longer alone on the path. Ahead, I can just make out two low voices, locked in what sounds like a heated argument.

My steps slow as I quickly slip my mask over my face again. One quick glance about confirms that there is nowhere for me to hide to avoid those ahead. This portion of the trail is far too treacherous for that, having been cut straight into the side of a sheer cliff.

I step closer to the edge to look over it, only for bits of the earth beneath my feet to crumble away and cascade to the forest far below.

I have no choice but to confront whoever is foolish enough to find themselves on this path. Moving toward the voices, my shadows gather around me, as I ready myself for whatever is to come.

Rounding the bend, I come to a standstill as I take in the two figures before me. There is barely an inch between their faces as they row, their fists clenched at their sides as they near their breaking points.

"Eros?" I say in surprise, my gaze shifting between him and Cerberus. The two men glance up at me, one frowning as the other gives me a smug look.

If Eros is here, then Hazel must be nearby. My heart thuds in my chest, my fury at him for dragging her to a place like this quickly replaced by my eagerness to lay eyes on her.

Only, as I peer past him, I realize that they are alone. My shadows surge forward, but her presence is nowhere to be found.

"See, I told you," Cerberus growls at Eros.

Eros shoves Cerberus in the chest, nearly sending him over the edge of the cliff before stepping toward me.

His mouth opens, but I hold up a hand to cut off whatever flowery excuse he is about to sprout.

My shadows whip around him in warning, and he frowns but slowly closes his mouth.

"Where is she?" I growl, darkness filling in around us as I take another step forward. "Where is Hazel? What have you done with her?"

"Done with her?" Eros laughs, though he has the good sense to sound nervous now that we are no longer playing by the rules of his palace. "I have done nothing, though I wholeheartedly wish that was not true."

The look that crosses his face as he says this makes me want nothing more than to throw him over the cliff, but I resist the urge. Instead, I take another step toward Eros, towering over him as I draw myself up to my full height.

"Then, where is she?" I demand, my voice low and dangerous. "Why is she not by your side?"

Inky shadows swell up around me, my rage growing with each passing second, when Cerberus suddenly steps between the two of us.

"Move," I order, but Cerberus only shifts into his hellhound, hackles raised and teeth bared in warning. My fists clench at my sides as I glance from him to Eros. "What is the meaning of this?"

"I needed his help," Eros answers, "to find you."

"Why?" I ask, my eyes narrowing on him. It is only now that I notice his disheveled appearance and fear finally begins to set in. "Hazel. Tell me, now, what has happened to her!"

"She was taken."

"Taken? By whom?" I demand, my shadows coiling around me in anger.

"Hades."

"What?" My heart drops at his words, dread settling like a lead weight in my stomach.

"She was not the only one taken," the pale god hurries to add. "It appears that he may be searching for the woman from the ball."

Silence falls as I try to process what he is telling me, but my mood only darkens as I realize what this means.

His little plan worked too well. Hades will not rest until he has made Hazel his.

"Damn you, Eros! You were meant to protect her! I should have known better than to trust you—"

"I *was* protecting her," Eros shouts, huge white wings springing from his back as he shoves Cerberus aside. "I am *trying* to—"

"Her absence begs to differ," I say, cutting him off, my voice calm even as my shadows betray my wrath. They dart out at him, but he leaps out of the way, his wings sending a cloud of dust up around us.

"Tell me, how could I go up against Hades?" Eros calls out. "I am no match against him, and if I had done so ... if I had shown my hand, revealed the mortal's importance to me, I would not have been able to seek you out. It would have only put her in more danger than she is now. I came to you because," Eros says, his jaw working as he settles on the path once again and takes a tentative step forward, "because I need your help, Death."

Though rage still courses through my veins, my

shadows calm at the desperation in his voice. As much as I hate to admit it, Eros is right.

I take a deep breath, trying to quell the anger that still boils within me, I cannot let my emotions get the best of me.

Not now.

Not while Hazel is in such imminent danger.

"Come, we must make haste before it is too late," I say even as Cerberus once again blocks my path, shifting back into his human form.

"Not so fast."

"Move, or I *will* throw you from this cliff."

"Not before you tell me why this mortal is worth all this trouble to you in the first place."

"Because she is *everything*," I snarl. "Everything this damned world seems to have forgotten. She is all that is good, all that is worth living for. She is a light in an eternal abyss of darkness … because Hazel's life is worth a thousand times more than any being I have ever known to walk this realm or hers."

Cerberus does not flinch at the ice in my voice, but I see the way his eyes brighten with a curiosity that I do not like. I said too much, and I do not know why I felt the need to explain anything to the beast in the first place.

"Move, Cerberus."

Hades' dog watches me for a moment longer before stepping out of my way, motioning for me to pass. I narrow my eyes on him as he gives me a mocking bow of his head before striding past him.

Eros quickly steps into place behind me, Cerberus

taking up the rear as I lead the way down the path and back to the Aglaia.

All too soon, Eros cannot help but fill the silence as he overexplains everything that has happened since I so foolishly left Hazel alone with him. Apparently, Hazel is not the only woman still trapped within the walls of Hades' palace, though I struggle to understand the reasoning behind this.

"There are many who are," Eros pauses, clearing his throat as he remembers who follows behind us, "less than pleased with the king's conduct, as of late. Or, so I have heard."

It would seem that Hades has finally stretched the limits of his power too far. Perhaps this is just the edge we need to challenge him. But how?

"We need a plan," I say, cutting Eros off as he trails off on some tangent about pleasure and appeasing the other gods. "Preferably one that does not require the involvement of fickle gods."

"Perhaps we only appear fickle to one who does not have to regularly deal with the workings of this realm," Eros retorts, taking me by surprise.

I turn on my heel to give him a hard look.

"Speak clearly."

"You have not been here," the pale god says, drawing closer. "You have not seen nor had to endure the atrocities that have been wrought upon us. We do what we must to survive, and we take what little pleasure we can from it. How could you, who does not have to answer to any king, understand?"

"I understand far better than you know."

"*Only* because of the girl, and only just a taste at that."

Cerberus glances between us as my fists clench at my sides, but then I let out a ragged sigh. Again, Eros is not wrong. If it were not for Hazel, I could have gone the rest of eternity without visiting this hellhole.

Let alone allowing Hades any authority over my actions. If it were not for Hazel, I would have slaughtered him and half the court the moment he refused to open the gates.

And given what I have just learned, I still might, but I do not have time to argue this fact with Eros.

The gods and their lives here are none of my concern. Hazel is.

Turning, I storm off, forcing Eros and Cerberus to scramble to keep pace with me.

However begrudgingly.

Stepping into the city, the tension that has been left to brew is palpable. The streets are unusually empty as we move through them, and yet this does nothing to lessen the heaviness in the air.

I lift my gaze to fix it on the sapphire palace, my lip curling up over my teeth as I set off toward it, only to have Cerberus step into my path again.

"Get out of my way," I growl.

"Listen," he says, "you cannot simply storm into the palace."

"I can, and I will—"

"Do you *want* him to kill her?"

"Of course not," I snarl.

"Then give me a chance to find out what is happening."

"No."

"Unlike you, I can get into the palace without any questions being asked," Cerberus hisses, placing the palm of his hand on my chest to stop me from moving around him. "Let me see what, if anything, he has done with the mortal, before you cause a bigger problem here than there already is."

"You are *loyal* to Hades," I say coldly. "Do not think I have forgotten this fact so easily. Why should I trust you to do anything of the sort?"

"I never said you should trust me," he answers, sneering as he cocks his head to one side. "Besides you of all beings should know why that is. Still, if it helps, I swear on that very loyalty that I will do as I have said and return to you with whatever it is I find out."

"Why?"

"Curiosity," Cerberus says with a shrug. "I want to know for myself what kind of mortal is capable of bringing Death to his knees for her."

"And after you find out whatever it is you wish to learn, what then?"

"I shall make my own decision when the time comes."

"No."

"Death," Eros presses, "this may be the only way of rescuing her without casualty."

"I do not care."

"I am speaking in regard to *her* life. Her soul. The

moment you go after her, Hades will wield her like a weapon."

"He is already doing so by keeping her from me."

"Yes, but if Cerberus can find out why and where she is being kept, we may stand a chance of rescuing her without bloodshed."

I narrow my eyes at him, weighing my options. It is true that I cannot simply storm into the palace without a plan, but I did have a plan, albeit a bloodthirsty one ... as Eros seems to have surmised.

"Fine," I say through gritted teeth, "but you have one night before I slaughter the entirety of this kingdom to get to her, and if I so much as hear that she has been harmed ... *nothing* will stop me from exacting my revenge upon this realm and your master."

"One night is all I need," he says after a moment of tense silence. Then, without another word, he bounds off toward Hades' palace.

I watch him disappear around a corner before turning back to Eros.

"I suppose this is the part where I invite you back to my place," he says with a cocky grin that elicits an annoyed growl from me.

I wave him on, hoping that we can come up with a plan to rescue Hazel before I am forced to make good on my threat.

A threat that, with Hades' deal with the Fates still intact, would most likely bring ruin to us all.

15

HAZEL

Unsurprisingly, I'm yet again left completely alone in my room for the rest of the day.

No one comes to bring food or water or to escort me to the dining room. I don't even hear so much as a footstep in the halls outside the locked door.

It's only when it starts to feel as though I've been forgotten, lost to the nothingness of the palace that I suddenly remember the package. Racing into the bathroom, I'm relieved to find the bundle of fabric where I left it.

Dropping to my knees, I quickly pull the bundle from within. As I peel back the brown parchment, the small book Cyprian gave me falls into my lap. I hardly dare to believe it's really here as I stare down at it for a long moment.

Carefully, I pick it up and flip it open, only to see that the page with the small illustration has been torn out. Sighing, my shoulders sag as I trace the jagged edge of the paper with one finger.

I don't know what I was expecting, but it wasn't this. This heartache, this overwhelming pain that accompanies the sight of the torn page. As I stare at it, Lilia's words from the night before come to mind.

Frowning, I can't help but wonder if I made a terrible mistake with Death over such a small thing. Perhaps I was too quick to judge his intentions... but then I shake the thought from my mind.

As much as I want to believe that, I saw my father *here* in the Underworld with my very own eyes. The book is one thing, but my father's life?

No.

If Death cannot prove he kept our deal, then it does not matter how much I love him. I cannot be with someone like that.

Grabbing the parchment paper, I rise and return to the bedroom. Re-wrapping the book, I tuck it under the mattress, unwilling to be caught with it out and have it taken away. I still need ink to write a note, but at least I'm one step closer.

Lying down, I stare up at the dark ceiling as I allow myself to get lost in thought.

Despite my best efforts, my mind keeps returning to Death. My heart aches as I try but fail to keep myself from imagining a future with him. As much as I want to save my father, my own life means nothing without Death.

Perhaps, in some ways, this is easier. I care little for my mortal life now, not when all that I love is no more.

Sitting up, I chide myself.

Life with Death was never a possibility. It has only

ever been a dream. Even if we succeeded here, and I was returned to my body, I am *mortal*. We wouldn't grow old, let alone share a life together.

Even if we could somehow share my life, it would be him watching me age, and eventually die. My body no longer capable of housing my soul.

In the end, it would always be death.

I shouldn't even pretend to allow myself to daydream about a different life. My mind spinning, I get up to pace the room as I try to refocus on the task at hand. I'm supposed to be finding a way to save my father, not bemoaning my poor life choices.

I glance at the window, suddenly realizing it's grown dark.

I pause in my pacing and wander over to the window, peering out at the starless sky. The darkness outside seems to mirror the hopelessness I feel in my heart.

My stomach growls softly, informing me of its displeasure at being ignored. Pressing a hand to it, I give it a firm shush. I can still remember the times that I went to bed starving, I can last longer than this if that's the game Hades plans on playing.

Still, my stomach lets out another growl of hunger.

"Hush," I whisper. "I will not be undone by you."

Just then, another growl seems to fill the room ... only this one doesn't come from my stomach.

I freeze at the sound, the hairs on the back of my neck standing on end. Slowly, I turn to face the door. From just outside my room comes another low growl, followed by the sound of low sniffing, as if some large creature is prowling just outside it.

Immediately, my heart swells as I recall Eros' ability to shift. He's found me. By some miracle, he's managed to make his way into Hades' palace and find me.

Hope floods through me as I take an excited step toward the door, just as a key is inserted and turned in the lock. A smile is already forming on my lips as the door opens to reveal not a creature nor Eros ... but a man I have never seen before.

He is as beautiful as he is terrifying as he fills the entirety of the doorframe. Messy dark hair is pushed back from a powerful face, complete with thick brows and full lips. Broad-shouldered, he is strong but lean, cut to athletic perfection, as he leans into the room, his sharp eyes searching the space before finally landing on me.

I stop in my tracks, my smile faltering and my heart skipping a nervous beat in my chest.

"Who are you?"

He doesn't answer, his head cocking to one side as he continues to stare at me with eyes that almost seem to ignite and burn from within. I take a step back, watching as his brow furrows.

Without a word, he ducks to step into the room.

"Who are you?" I repeat, my voice slightly louder this time.

He still doesn't answer, but instead takes another step towards me. I can already feel the heat radiating off of him, and it sends a cold shiver racing down my spine even as a thin layer of sweat beads across my skin.

"I demand you tell me who you are."

He pauses at this, his eyebrow lifting.

"I should be the one asking who you are," he finally replies, his deep voice filling the room.

"What do you mean?" I ask.

"How is it that you, a mere mortal, have managed to beguile Death himself, not to mention Eros and the very king of the Underworld."

I swallow hard as I take in the stranger's words. How does he know about my connection to Death and the others? Is he an ally or an enemy? My mind races with questions as I try to assess the situation.

"You must be mistaken," I say, "I have beguiled no one, at least, it was never my intention to do so ... I am simply trying to save my father's life."

His eyes narrow on me, and I find myself unable to look away. Something about him seems familiar, but I am certain I've never seen this man before.

"Curious," he mutters, his voice so low that I'm not sure I was meant to hear it.

Taking another step toward me, he cocks his head to the other side, the sudden motion causing his dark hair to flop playfully across his forehead. In a split second, he's gone from a terrifying monster to looking more like a puppy with ears too big for its head.

"What could you know about Death and Eros' feelings?" I ask, taking a small step back. "Why are you here? What business do you have with me?"

He snorts at this.

"Business with you? None. But your connection to Death and the others is of great interest to me," he says, taking yet another step closer to me. His eyes roam over my body, and I feel exposed under his intense scrutiny.

"There is something about you that draws them in, something that makes them see you as more than just a mere mortal. I want to know what that is."

"But how do you know this?"

"How could I not know when you are all they talk about? Besides, your scent was all over them, they could only ever mean you."

"You were with them?" I ask, my cheeks flushing and my heart skipping another beat in my chest as I realize what Eros must have done. Then I take another step back as he moves further into the room. I'm nearly pressed against the wall at this point, unable to place more distance between us.

"Unfortunately. Now, tell me, tiny human, how do you do it?"

Again, he cocks his head to the other side, the motion unnerving in its sharpness ... but then the dim light glints off something in his ear.

A sapphire earring.

Why does he seem so familiar?

Blinking, I begin to piece together who this man may be.

We *have* met before, but not in this form.

"Cerberus," I breathe.

"So, you have figured it out," he says with a rakish grin that reveals sharp canines, taking another step toward me.

"Cerberus. Cerberus, stay!" I order as the distance between us becomes uncomfortably close.

I don't know what comes over me to think I have any authority to order him about, but it does not stop me from trying. Straightening, I point toward his feet and repeat my words, this time more firmly.

Immediately, his steps falter.

His eyes widen slightly as if he's just as surprised by this as I am. Cerberus looks down at his feet and then back up at me, something in them sparking a fire deep within me ...

And apparently, within him as well.

16

HAZEL

Cerberus lets out a low growl, his eyes now fixed intently on mine. The fire that lights them is warm, glowing through him as his lips pull into a rakish grin. For a second, I am sure that I must be imagining what I'm seeing, but as he tilts his head, I realize this man has actual fire burning within the very depths of his being.

And it's growing hotter with each passing second.

The air around us crackles with an electrifying tension, and I can feel my heartbeat quickening.

"Say that again," he demands, his voice low and reverberating through me as he takes another step toward me.

I try to swallow past the lump that's taken root in my throat. Goosebumps prickle my skin as I try to find some thread of courage to give him another command. But it's almost impossible to focus on anything other than the fire burning in his eyes.

My mouth opens, but not a single word manages to find its way past my lips.

Cerberus takes another step forward, his grin growing more devilish by the moment. He's far too close now, the heat of his body nearly unbearable in its intensity. Just as he moves to close the distance between us, I find my voice again.

"Stay," I command, the word coming out shaky. "Stay, Cerberus."

Cerberus lets out a low growl, but to my surprise, he stops in his tracks. He's so close now that I can smell him as waves of heat crash over me. His scent is a heady mix of musk, smoke, and something else I can't quite place.

I half expect to find displeasure in his face as our eyes meet again, but all I find is a strange sense of delight working its way over his features as he stares down at me from his great height.

A shiver works its way across his shoulders and down his spine just before his fingertips burst into fire, golden flames licking their way up his arms. His hair and eyes spark, becoming edged in flames as a soft sound of pleasure escapes Cerberus' lips.

He leans forward, one massive hand flattening against the stone just beside my head. I hardly know what to do as I press myself flatter against the wall, pinned here by a man literally on fire as scorching heat radiates from him.

I blink up at Cerberus, his smoky scent filling my nose as my heart begins to race.

Neither of us says a word, and slowly the flames that cover him begin to retreat, leaving streaks of black soot across his skin in their wake. Cerberus bows his head as he reaches out to tilt my chin up, his fingertips nearly scorching me with lingering heat.

He pauses, his lips a hair's breadth from mine. So close I can nearly taste him, but then he pulls back. His brow furrowing for a moment as he straightens, the hunger that was in his eyes a moment before now replaced with something I can't quite figure out.

A soft smile, almost at odds with the devilish one from before, overtakes his face.

"Thank you," he says in a husky voice.

Surprised at this, I can't help but ask, "Thank you? For what?"

But, of course, he doesn't answer.

Instead, he takes a step back, looking me over with a disconcerting thoroughness before turning to exit the room without a word. I stare after him in shock. As the door closes behind him, the sound of the lock turning fills the room, finally startling me from my stupor.

What was *that*?

Tentatively, I move toward the door and press my ear to it, but there is nothing to hear. Cerberus is gone, and I am none the wiser as to why he was here in the first place, let alone who may have sent him.

If he hadn't mentioned Death and Eros, I would have certainly thought this was another one of Hades' games ... but now, I'm not so certain.

I turn from the door with a deep sigh. I could spend hours trying to piece together what just happened, and still be no closer to an answer.

Not that it matters anyway.

I am still no closer to escaping this place or saving my father than I was this morning.

But at least now, I have hope.

A weighty silence falls over the room as I lie in bed, unable to find sleep. I can't help but stare into the shadows, wishing that Death's form would take shape and step from them.

It must be close to midnight by the time I finally hear footsteps outside my door again. Sitting up, I am not surprised when the two guards from the night before step into my room.

Their faces are impassive as if they are here on a routine visit, but I know better. I can sense the underlying tension, the unspoken threat that hangs in the air between us.

One of the guards nods to me, indicating that I should get up and follow them. Again, not a word is spoken as I'm led through the palace back to the strange jungle room.

The other women are already gathered within the room by the time I arrive, but the mood is much more somber. It's hard to ignore as we wait to see what will be taught and expected of us tonight.

"Welcome back," Persephone says, her tone far from pleasant, as she once again appears in the pool of light that gathers in the center of the room.

Her eyes are hard, her smile too forced as she glances about the room. I'm still unsettled by this version of her as she begins to move about the room. Persephone stops in front of me and I can sense her eyes scouring my body. I try to meet her gaze but find myself looking away, intimidated by her unspoken power.

"You are all here again tonight for a very important lesson," she says, her voice low and dangerous. "One that may determine your fate in this realm. Tonight, you will learn about the power of submission."

I flinch as those around me lean in, eager to soak in every word she says.

"Hazel, come here," Persephone orders, once again singling me out.

I do my best to keep my emotions in check, though my heart thunders in my chest as I approach her. I can feel the other women's gazes boring into my back, watching my every move.

Persephone's hand snakes out, catching me by the chin and tilting my head up. Her eyes search mine, and I can feel a sense of triumph emanating from her.

"Submission is not weakness," she says, her voice low and silky. "It is power. The power to control and be controlled. The power to give yourself over completely to another and allow them to find pleasure in their perceived control."

Her hand falls away as she turns to face the other women.

"Your king, my husband, desires a queen who understands the value of submission. One who can willingly give herself over to him without him realizing power was exchanged. A woman to please him and satisfy his every desire. And tonight, I will teach you how to become that queen."

Persephone moves about the room, instructing us on different positions and techniques to please Hades and satisfy his desires. I feel sick to my stomach as I listen to her words. If she would just give me a moment of her time, then perhaps all these lessons would no longer be necessary ... but I know that, for now, I have no choice but to learn if I want a chance of surviving long enough to save my father.

Yet again, Persephone orders the others to practice on each other as she finishes demonstrating how to pleasure a man in ways I never even imagined. And, yet again, I am left standing awkwardly in the center of the room, watching on.

"That will be all for tonight," the queen announces. "It is time to choose tonight's seductress. Once more you will go to my husband to attempt to seduce him. But tonight, you are not wake him except by means of the pleasure I have just taught you."

Her eyes meet mine, and for one horrible moment, I think she means to select me. That tonight is the night I will be forced to seduce Hades. The very thought of giving myself over completely to him, to be at his beck and call, to be nothing more than a vessel for his pleasure, makes my skin crawl.

I can't do this, I—

"You," Persephone says, nodding to a woman just behind me.

I glance back to find a beautiful dark-haired woman, curvier than either Persephone or me, standing there. Her ample cleavage is on full display even as her cheeks flush with color.

Running a hand through her dark hair, she gives me a challenging look, and I almost think she's eager for this chance.

Of course, she probably is.

I suppose it's not every day that one finds themselves *invited* to seduce the God of the Underworld, and by his wife no less.

"Guards!" The woman holds her head high as the doors to the room open and Persephone's men file into the room. "Take this one to the king and return the rest to where you found them."

I watch as the chosen brunette is escorted quickly from the room, waiting for my own guards to appear by my side. Suddenly realizing this is may be my chance to speak with Persephone, I quickly turn toward her.

"Hazel, if you will stay," she says before I can open my mouth, "I would have a word with you."

I nod, trying to keep calm even as my heart leaps in my chest. My mind floods with everything I want to tell her as I wait for the others to leave.

Around me, the women slowly thin as they are led out of the room and back through the palace halls. Watching them, I can't help but notice the way each of them is careful to avoid meeting my eye. As the last of the women disappears from sight, my attention returns to Persephone.

"I—"

She holds up a hand to quiet me, and I reluctantly do as I'm bid.

Silence falls over the room, and I anxiously wait for her to break it. Several minutes pass, but she says nothing, her gaze lost in the leafy foliage that covers the ceiling.

Walking across the room, she settles onto a thick bed

135

of flowers at is seems to spring from nowhere. With a sigh, she plucks a soft pink flower, watching as its petals wither and fall to the floor.

I frown as she reaches for another and then another. Shifting slightly, the eerie light catches, sparkling over a trail of tears that's wet her cheek. Especially after the past two nights.

Another moment passes, and I find myself unable to stop the concern that tugs me closer as she curls up into a ball in the middle of the wilting petals.

"Persephone?"

She glances up at me, as if suddenly remembering she's not alone. All the ice and sharpness from before slowly melting from her face.

Letting out a sniffle, she pushes herself up into a sitting position and draws her knees to her chest.

"This is not the first time," she whispers.

I stare at her for a moment.

"What do you mean?"

"This is not the first time my husband's eyes have strayed. Hell, he has a whole harem of women at his beck and call," she says, her voice catching. "Each time I think it will be easier, but the pain has yet to lessen, and now ... and now *this*."

"I am so sorry," I say, my mouth going dry as I work up the courage to tell her everything. "I—"

"I am a *fool*, Hazel," Persephone interrupts, not seeming to hear me. "Despite it all, I love Hades. I hate him with all my heart, but yet, I find myself forced to love him. I am bound to him, trapped here in a web of false hope. I cannot escape him, and yet, I do not know if I even wish to."

I watch as Persephone falls silent once more, tears streaming down her face, and I hate that I have played any part in this pain.

Not knowing what else to say or do, I move toward her. She watches me as I settle down next to her and then tentatively wrap an arm around her shoulder.

The queen stiffens for a moment before turning to bury her face into my shoulder. Her entire body shakes with her sobs as I hold her. I hold Persephone close to me, feeling her pain and despair in every shuddering breath she takes.

For a moment, I forget why I'm here as we sit in silence, the only sounds in the room are her ragged breaths and the occasional sniffle. But then, a sudden realization hits me. This is my chance to help her, to free her from this loveless marriage.

Persephone suddenly pulls back, wiping the tears from her face with the back of her hand. She takes a deep breath, her eyes locking onto mine. My words catch on my tongue, and for a moment, I fear that she can see straight through me.

That she's realized I'm the one that's caused her husband's eye to stray yet again, though I never intended it to go this far.

"Thank you for being a true friend to me, Hazel," she says softly. "I am so sorry that you have been caught up in this mess. At least I know that I can trust you ... unlike the others who are all too eager for their chance to steal him away from me."

I cringe inwardly at this, guilt twisting its way into me like a dagger to the gut. Silence fills my ears to the point of ringing as I try to find the courage to explain to her what I've done.

What I was willing to do to save first my own life, and then my father's.

"Persephone—"

"Knowing you do not wish to seduce him is—"

"Persephone," I interrupt, as she turns to stare wide-eyed at me. "I need to tell you—"

Of course, the doors to the room slam open before another word can slip past my lips, and we both turn to see Deimos stride into the room.

"What is the meaning of this?" he snarls, several of Hades' guards filing into the room behind him along with a grinning, sharp-eyed woman.

Persephone leaps up, her fingers twitching with fury as little offshoots of vines burst from them in an endless cycle of life and death.

"Eris," the spring goddess says, quickly rising to her feet, "you are early."

"And a good thing too," Eris says, her gaze shifting to me. "You know none of these women are to be trusted. You cannot be left alone with them. Deimos, have the girl taken back to her room."

Deimos scowls at her order, but then signals for two of his men to grab me before I have a chance to protest. Persephone's jaw tightens, but she makes no move to stop them even as they drag me roughly away.

Yet again, I have failed.

17

CERBERUS

"I will do it."

Eros and Death both glance up at me.

Their stunned silence brings a slight smile to my lips as I move to join them in the courtyard. Death's shadows curl up around him as Eros continues to stare in my direction, his gaze not quite meeting my own.

"Really?" Eros asks

"What exactly are you agreeing to?" Death says, his voice quiet in its intensity.

It does not surprise me that he wants specifics. After all, he is the one whose life is comprised of deals.

Yet, I cannot help the annoyance that flares through me at the way he speaks to me, as if I am nothing more than another mortal come to throw my soul at him.

"I will help you reunite with the mortal girl."

"*Hazel*," Death corrects. "Does this also mean you will help us leave the Underworld?"

My body tenses at this; the very thought of the mortal leaving this realm sends a wave of displeasure coursing through me. I hesitate for a moment, doing my best to ignore the weight of Death's glower as I consider.

"I cannot agree to anything of the sort," I answer. "Not yet."

"Why not?" Death asks.

"Because whether you like it or not, Hades still holds the key, and he is still my master."

"Then what is the point of you helping us?"

"I have my reasons."

"Cerberus," Death growls, stepping closer. "What are you not telling me?"

"I simply wish to get to know her better before I decide. Is that too much to ask?"

Death narrows his eyes at me, his suspicion palpable. I can feel the tension radiating off him in waves, but I refuse to back down. After all, I am not just some pawn to be used and discarded at his whim.

Eros, on the other hand, seems to be the only one who is not affected by the tension between us. He takes a step forward, his head cocking to one side.

"You like her," he says.

I grit my teeth, refusing to acknowledge his words. I am not like the mortals, who are easily swayed by their emotions.

"What?" Death hisses, his eyes darkening behind his mask. "Is this true?"

"I find her intriguing," I admit.

"You better not have laid a single finger on her," Death warns.

I snort before replying, "At least my touch will not kill

her. Really, if anyone should be warned off touching her, it is you."

Death moves to close the distance between us, his shadows swirling up around him as his rage builds, but Eros steps between us before he can lunge.

"Now is not the time to fight among ourselves," he shouts. "If Cerberus is willing to help, then I think we should accept it."

I blink, only just now realizing I had shifted in order to take on Death ... over a mere mortal.

How strange.

Death remains where he is for a moment longer before letting out a deep sigh.

"Of course," he says, taking a step back, and I return to my human form. "Very well, then, how exactly do you intend to help?"

I grin at this before saying, "I can start by telling you exactly where Hades is keeping her."

"Well?" Eros presses as Death tenses, shifting forward slightly as if worried he will miss what I have to say, and I cannot deny I like the power I hold in this moment.

"Speak, Cerberus."

"She is being kept in the tallest tower of the East wing, in a room all by herself."

"Why? Where are the other women?"

"I do not know why, as I have yet to speak with Hades," I answer, "but the others are being kept together in the servants' wing."

"She is alone ... are you certain of it?" Eros asks.

"Yes, at least when she is not being summoned by Hades or Persephone."

"Eros, what are you thinking?" Death asks warily as the pale god turns to walk away.

"I need to ask her about her brother."

"Her brother? What are you talking about?"

Eros pauses, slowly turning to face us, his expression stricken.

"There was a soul at the gate," he says as Death's gaze fixes on him. "He said he was her brother."

"What?! And you did not think to say something to me? Damn you, Eros!"

Death lunges at him, but before can get close enough to grab him, Eros shifts into a tiny white bird and takes to the air. I watch as he flits about the garden, dodging Death's shadows as they trail after him, before finally disappearing in the direction of Hades' palace.

Slowly, I turn to look back at Death, his chest heaving in rage and frustration. As his gaze meets mine, I shoot a grin his way.

"Did you know about this?"

"No, but I can certainly use it to our advantage."

Death's eyes narrow on me. "What are you planning?"

"Well, I suggest you go find out more about this supposed brother," I answer, my grin widening. "As for me, I am about to be instated as the mortal's personal guard."

18

HAZEL

I toss and turn as sleep evades me. Guilt makes for a heavy weight as I struggle to find solace in sleep.

Of course, I don't want to bed Hades ... I don't even want to pretend that I do anymore. Yet, I don't know what else I'm supposed to do if I cannot find a way to speak to Persephone. To tell her the truth of everything.

Maybe, just maybe, she can find it in her heart to forgive me and help find a way out of this mess before it's too late.

Before I have no choice but to actually take Hades to bed.

No, I can't allow myself to even think that will happen. I have to believe that Eros, perhaps even Death, will come for me before then.

With this small blossom of hope growing in my chest, I finally manage to fall into a fitful sleep.

I wake sometime later to the feeling that I am being watched. Sitting up, I rub the sleep from my eyes as I peer about the room.

Early morning light casts an eerie glow on everything, leaving me more than a little unsettled as the shadows morph with my imagination ... but there's no one here.

Just as I'm about to discount the feeling and try to fall back asleep, I hear the sound of light tapping on the glass. Turning to look toward the window, I spot a tiny white bird perched just outside.

Slowly getting out of bed, I make my way to the window, watching the bird closely as I try not to frighten it. It's small enough to fit in the palm of my hand, with feathers as white as snow.

As I move closer, it flutters its wings and hops several times on the windowsill, tilting its head to each side as if it's trying to tell me something. Unlatching the window, I gently push it open and reach out my hand.

To my surprise, the bird immediately hops onto my finger, its small talons barely grazing my skin as it begins to chirp softly at me. I push the window open further, carefully drawing my hand back inside the room.

Suddenly, the chirping becomes more urgent and the bird leaps off my finger to instantly be replaced by the much more familiar form of Eros. He barely has time to straighten before I've thrown my arms around him.

His body tenses before he wraps me in the safety of his own arms, holding me tightly. Tears spill out onto my cheeks as emotions choke the back of my throat, keeping all my questions from tumbling out of me.

I cling to him, hardly daring to believe he's really

here. That against every odd he's found a way to get to me ... and afraid that if I let go, it'll all be but a dream.

He pulls back slightly, reaching to tilt my face toward his as he searches me with his pale eyes. Instantly, I feel energy pulled from me as his skin meets mine.

"Are you alright?" he asks softly, his thumb brushing away a stray tear. I nod, unable to trust my voice. "Good."

Before I can say anything, his lips meet mine and all words are lost to me in the heady rush of emotions that hits me, draining me of myself. What little energy I have is nearly washed away as my knees buckle beneath me.

His arms tighten, keeping me upright and anchored to him as he deepens our kiss, and I find myself struggling not to get lost in him. Vaguely, I'm aware of Eros walking me backward, the back of my legs hitting the edge of the bed.

His weight covers me as we collapse onto the bed, his hands moving along my curves. Eros' desire for me suddenly deepens, his touch igniting a fire so hot within me I almost cry out in pain, as he pulls at my nightgown ... and I'm abruptly brought back to my senses.

My body freezes, and it takes him a moment to realize before he pulls back. My cheeks burn with shame as I find myself unable to look him in the face.

"I can't," I whisper.

"I apologize. I should not have started anything," Eros says, pulling back as he runs a hand through his hair. "Least of all when you are in so much danger."

"How did you find me?"

"Cerberus."

I stare at him dumbfounded for a long moment. "Then he is helping us?"

"I would not go so far as to say that. Not just yet, anyway."

"Of course. Well, what are we waiting for?" I ask. "You are here to take me away, right?"

"No, not yet," he says, his voice hesitant.

My heart sinks at his words. "Why not?"

Eros doesn't answer immediately, instead choosing to move to sit on the edge of the bed.

"It is quite impossible, at the moment. At least until we can find a way to convince Hades to release you, or escape through the palace itself."

"Can't you fly me out of here?"

"No, Persephone and Cerberus are among the only beings aside from Hades who retain their powers within these walls," Eros says before practically spitting, "and Deimos."

"But the sparrow ..."

"Minute magic, as is allowed within a certain range of the palace," he explains. "And, as you saw, I was unable to keep that form as soon as you pulled me into the room."

Frowning, I can't help but ask, "Then why are you here?"

"To give you hope," Eros answers. "To let you know that we have not given up, and to remind you that you are not alone. We are working on a plan to get you out of here."

"Who do you mean by *we*?"

Eros pauses at this before carefully saying, "Death, myself, and now, to a much lesser extent, Cerberus."

"So, Death is here? In Aglaia?"

"Yes."

"Then why hasn't he come for me?"

"I convinced him to wait until we can come up with a decent plan."

"But he is Death—" I start.

"Exactly. He is *death*. He cannot simply barge in without putting the entire kingdom, and your very life in danger. It would be a bloodbath unlike anything ever seen, and it is unlikely that anyone would survi—" Eros begins to explain, but he gets no further as the sound of a key scraping in the lock fills the room.

Before either of us can move, the door bursts open to reveal Cerberus' towering frame, his eyes moving from Eros to me.

"There," Cerberus says, "I told you that Eros would stop at nothing to try to steal her away from you."

Ducking to enter the room, he steps to one side to reveal a scowling Hades, his hair alight with blue fire, standing behind him.

"Seize him."

"No," I cry as several guards push their way into the room at Hades' order.

The guards grab him, and he struggles against them, but it is no use as they pull him off the bed and away from me. I watch as his gaze narrows on Cerberus, who just smirks back at him, and my stomach twists with disgust.

I should have known better than to think trusting him was ever an option.

"Please," I beg Hades, as I step toward him. "Please,

have mercy on Eros, he was only here to make sure I was okay. He wasn't trying to steal me away."

Hades ignores my pleas as he watches the guards drag the pale god out into the hallway. Once Eros is removed from the room, Hades shuts the door and turns to face Cerberus again.

They ignore me, Hades nodding once to Cerberus as tears slip from my eyes.

"You were right to come to me with this, Cerberus," Hades says. "I knew you were loyal, but you have outdone yourself this time. Now, tell me. What reward would you like for this? Simply name it and it shall be yours."

Cerberus pauses to mull this over for a second before his gaze shifts to me.

"Thank you, my king. If it would please you, I would like nothing more than to do my duty by you. Allow me to take over as the mortal's watch, to make sure no one else attempts to come for her."

"Hmm," Hades says, eyeing Cerberus for a moment. "Very well. From this moment on, I entrust her care to you. You will be her keeper, ensuring she remains safely here until I state otherwise."

"Of course, my king," Cerberus says with a bow of his head.

Hades starts toward the door only to stop and turn back to look at me. I meet his gaze, not caring to hide my anger or frustration as I stare up at him.

"And you," he says, giving me a once over, his expression strange. "You will be joining me for dinner tonight ... alone. See to it that you make yourself presentable."

Before I can reply, not that I think it would do any

good, Hades has thrown open the door and swept from the room. I watch him disappear before slowly turning to glare at Cerberus as we're left standing alone in my room.

I scowl at him, even as a mischievous smile pulls at the corner of his lips. The silence stretches between us, and yet he only seems to grow more amused by the moment.

Finally, I can't take it any longer.

"What have you done?" I hiss. "What will Hades do to Eros? I suppose I shouldn't be so shocked to find that you can be as cruel and cold as your master, but I had hoped ..."

I trail off as confusion contorts his face, and he cocks his head to one side.

"What?" I demand as he remains quiet.

"He will be brought to the dungeons to await punishment," he explains. "As is fitting for anyone who tries to steal from the king."

"Why?"

Cerberus frowns at this, though mischief seems to burn within his eyes at my annoyance.

"I have simply done my duty," he answers. "It was Eros who was caught crossing a line. Who knows what he would have done with you, had I not led Hades here. Now I can make sure that you are looked after and properly guarded as my master decides how best to handle you."

"How did you even know Eros would be here?" I ask, my eyes narrowing as I take a step toward him. "He flew in as a small bird, so how exactly did you know that you would find him here?"

Of course, I already know how, but I want him to admit that he betrayed Eros. That he is not to be trusted.

The mischief dies in his eyes as he stares at me; his silence is all I need to know that he would rather not have this discussion.

But I want him to admit it.

I need him to.

"Cerberus," I say. "How did you know that Eros would be here? Tell me."

Again, I am surprised by the command in my voice, but I don't back down.

"Because I told him where to find you," he answers without hesitation, almost as if he's suddenly eager to answer. His eyes widen in surprise as the words leave his mouth. Then they narrow on me as he takes a threatening step toward me. "What are these dark powers of yours, mortal?"

Dark powers?

Confusion washes over me as I stare up at him. I open my mouth to try to answer but realize that I have no explanation to offer. He watches me for a moment longer before snorting and turning on his heel.

"Clean up, I will be back to collect you for dinner."

With that, he storms out of the room, slamming and locking the door behind him before I have a chance to mutter another word.

19

CERBERUS

Shivers of pleasure run up and down my spine, and I am forced to physically shake them off as I make my way down the tower stairs and away from the tiny mortal.

If she is, in fact, mortal at all.

I do not understand what has come over me, but I cannot push her from my mind. Nor do I not want to.

One command, and I wanted nothing more than to obey.

Two, and I wanted to lay down my life for her.

A single touch, and I knew I was hers.

With Hades being my master, I have to careful not to reveal this bond to him. I am not supposed to be able to form fated bonds, or so I had been led to believe.

But obviously, that is not the case.

Still, Hades must continue to believe that I am loyal to him, and only him.

And as for the mortal, I must do my best not to let her discover the hold she has on me.

At least, for the time being.

She must be innocent if ...

When I am forced to betray my king for her.

My fated mate.

20

HAZEL

As expected, I am left to my own devices for the rest of the day. My mind spins as I pace back and forth across the room, mulling over everything that's happened so far.

Worry eats away at me as my thoughts turn to Eros. I can't help but picture him locked away in a damp cell, bruised and beaten, as he awaits his punishment. Everything seems so much worse now that I know even the gods seem capable of dying.

Whatever an immortal death entails.

It's all just another reminder of how out of my depths I am here.

I also need to be wary of Cerberus, as far as I can tell, he is *not* to be trusted. I cannot begin to imagine what made Eros think it possible in the first place.

The hellhound is even more dangerous than I would have guessed. Especially with his obvious desire to please his master ... whatever the cost.

Frustrated, and nearly driven mad by my own

thoughts, I turn back to the bed and reach under the mattress to pull out my hidden book. Leaving the parchment behind, I settle on the floor by the window to try to read in an effort to distract myself.

Opening it, I close my eyes as I lift the book to my nose, breathing in the warm, well-loved scent of the worn pages. Sighing, I lean back against the wall and turn to the first story.

Though it takes several minutes to lose myself within the words, I soon find my heart and mind calming as the stories carry me far, far away from here. The book was obviously meant for a young girl, but the fairytales still manage to bring a smile to my face; however bittersweet.

I inhale sharply, peering about the dim light of the room as my mind scrambles to remember where I am. Glancing down, I realize I must have fallen asleep, the book of fairytales laying half-open in my hand on the floor beside me ... and a blanket tucked in around my waist.

My heart leaps in my chest as I realize that someone must have come in while I was sleeping. Before this thought has time to settle, I'm suddenly reminded of Hades' no-so-optional invitation to dinner.

Panic crashes through me as I throw the blanket off and pull myself up onto my feet. Looking out the window, I groan in frustration.

I don't have much time.

Hurrying across the room, I quickly re-wrap my book and stuff it under the mattress, muttering a grateful prayer that whoever came in didn't take it. It's only as I straighten that I realize a new dress has been lain out on the bed for me.

At least I know what I'll be wearing.

Grabbing it, I make my way into the bathroom, quickly stripping off my nightgown and sinking into the steaming waters of the bath. I viciously scrub at my skin and hair, as I rush to clean myself as best I can before I'm sent for.

Stepping out of the bath, I wrap a towel around myself just as I catch a glimpse of my reflection in the mirror and can't help but sigh.

I look even less alive than I feel. Wet hair hangs in a tangled mess around me; my face is sallow and making my dark circles appear more prominent than ever before. The lack of food and good sleep certainly isn't helping my cause.

Turning away from my reflection, I finish towel drying before pulling on the new dress. Again, it's a dark midnight blue, but this time it also has intricate silver detailing that catches in the light, however dim, and makes it sparkle like a starlight night.

I'm almost shocked by how modest the dress is, but not at all displeased. The last thing I want right now is to try to seduce Hades. This may be the one chance I get to spend time with him on my own, and yet I can't seem to bring myself to care.

Not after everything I just learned from Eros.

I need more time to plan, to hope that Death will come and prove me wrong before it's too late to save myself.

Braiding my hair, I take one last look at my reflection

before perching on the edge of the bed to wait. I don't have to wait more than a few minutes before the door opens.

Cerberus ducks inside, ready to escort me to dinner as promised.

"Come."

I stare at him for a long moment before rising to obey and nervously smoothing out the skirt of my dress. Suddenly, I wonder if I've made a mistake not trying to make myself more presentable.

"You look lovely," Cerberus comments as if reading my mind, and I glance up at him in surprise. "The dress suits you. Now, come."

I say nothing in response, unwilling to waste any more words on him. This seems like the safest route, given that he might as well be Hades' eyes and ears.

Yet, he seems eager to strike up a conversation with me as we leave my room behind.

"What do you think of the palace?" he asks, as we make our way down the stairs. Again, I don't say anything. I can feel his gaze shift to me, but I keep my eyes fixed forward and my head held high as we move.

He lets out a small snort of annoyance, and I have to fight back a small smile at this unexpected prize. We walk on in blessed silence for a few minutes before he speaks again.

"I hope the blanket was enough to keep you warm."

"That was you?" I ask, unable to stop the question from slipping past my lips.

He grins at this, his sharp canines glinting in the light, and I realize I've just given him exactly what he wanted.

Pressing my lips firmly together, I train my eyes forward again, determined not to speak to him again.

Of course, this doesn't stop him from talking to me. He tells me about his day, the errands he was sent on, and the beings he met. I try not to ignore him, but I can't help myself. Cerberus' day seems almost entirely consumed with carrying out Hades' every menial demand.

Peeking up at him, I frown as I wonder why this massive creature would allow Hades to treat him more like a working dog than a trusted companion. Though, I suppose he is a hellhound.

It's only when we turn down a hallway and up a new set of winding stairs that I realize I'm not being taken to the main dining room. Instead, Cerberus stops outside a new set of doors. Pushing them open for me, he steps aside to allow me entry into a much more private room.

There's a table in the center of the room set for two. Hades stands behind a chair, one hand gripping the back and an impatient look on his face. Behind him, is a large open balcony that looks out on the bustling Underworld, and for a moment I'm lost in the scenery.

"Leave us," Hades says, dismissing Cerberus with a wave of his hand.

I find myself more than a little shocked by the rudeness with which he speaks to perhaps his most loyal subject, and I can't help but glance up at my guard. His silence feels odd after all the talking he did on the walk over.

With a nod toward Hades, he leaves; but not before shooting a strange look my way. The doors are pulled shut behind him, and I turn back to Hades feeling more perplexed than ever.

"Come, join me," Hades orders, motioning toward the chair across from where he stands.

I do as I'm told and quickly take my seat. He joins me at the table, and I can't help but glance about the room.

The table is simple, but elegant, with a black table-cloth and silver plates. A decanter of deep red wine sits in the center of the table, surrounded by untouched platters of beautifully plated food. The room is dimly lit, the only source of light coming from the candles that flicker throughout the room, and the strange glow of the darkening Underworld through the open balcony doors.

We're completely alone here, and I instantly find myself missing the presence of the other women. Even a guard would be a welcome sight.

"Will no one else be joining us?" I ask after a moment of silence.

Hades says nothing as he moves to pour me a glass of wine.

I stare at the bright red liquid as it fills the glass. It reminds me of blood and I'm unable to bring myself to reach for it, even as he pours himself a glass and raises it to his lips.

His eyes remain fixed on me over the rim of his glass as I sit nearly frozen in my chair. Lowering the glass, he motions at the food before me.

"Eat."

I glance down, taking in the bread, cheeses, roasted meats, and vegetables. They look amazing, but I suddenly find I have no appetite, not when I can feel his eyes watching my every move.

Meeting his gaze, he raises an eyebrow as if expecting me to challenge him on this.

It's not like I really have a choice, anyway. I need sustenance, if my earlier reflection is anything to go by, and I *am* here to dine with him. Hopefully, the sooner the meal is finished, the sooner I can retreat back to my room.

I take small nibbles, barely tasting the food.

Hades doesn't eat. Instead, he leans back in his chair, watching me as he sips from the glass of wine in his hand.

My stomach grows tighter with each passing moment, making the process of eating that much harder. I'm not sure how I'm meant to finish the entire meal under his scrutiny. The silence seems to thicken around us, making it nearly unbearable to sit still.

"The dress Cerberus chose for you suits you," Hades says, his deep voice shattering the silence and startling me into dropping my fork.

I flinch at the jarring clink of it meeting my plate. Then, as slowly as I can, I glance up at Hades. He watches me, his eyes dark and calculating.

"Thank you," I force myself to mumble as politely as I can.

With a satisfied nod, he takes another sip from his glass.

My skin burns under his scrutiny, and I'm thrown off balance by his compliment.

"I find myself curious about you, mortal," he says, as

he finishes his glass. Shifting forward to set it down before leaning back in his chair and waving offhandedly at me. "Tell me about yourself. Tell me about the life you led before you found yourself in my kingdom."

Swallowing the food in my mouth, I reach for the wine. My throat is dry at the thought of speaking as I take a sip, the wine doing little to quench my sudden thirst. And yet, as I set the glass down, I feel as though I've just downed the entire bottle as my mouth opens and words begin to tumble from me.

He leans back in the chair, listening as I tell him about my life before Death and my arrival in the Under-world. In almost no time, I'm spilling nearly every little detail about myself. From learning to hold a paintbrush with my father's gentle guidance to the immense sadness of losing my mother.

The disappointment of Father remarrying, the endless torment my new family put me through, and how I came to stand before Death.

Nothing prior to my meeting of Death is held back, much to my own horror. Without any prompting, I tell him my fondest and my darkest memories. As the words finally dry on my tongue, I find myself exhausted from reliving the life I left behind.

My voice trails off as a soft sob overtakes me, my words still hanging in the air as if to taunt me over how pathetic my life was. Over how little I managed to achieve … and even then, I failed.

Even my death, the giving of my very soul, was not enough to save my father.

Tears sting the backs of my eyes, and I bury my face in my hands as I try to hide them.

Hades' chair scrapes against the floor, forcing me to look up, as he slowly rises. The measured tread of his boots against the marble floor echoes through the room as he makes his way over to me.

I blink up at him as I struggle to regain my composure, the tears in my eyes making him swim in my vision. I'm unable to read his expression as he leans down, cupping my chin in his massive hand as he tilts my face toward his.

"It appears there is more to you than meets the eye. What else are you not telling me, mortal?"

His eyes search my face for a moment as I try to think of an appropriate answer, but then I realize that's not what he's looking for as his eyes drop to my lips. I've barely had time to decipher the look that passes across his face before he bends and his lips find mine.

My shock only lasts a second before I pull away, using every ounce of strength and courage afforded to me. My chair topples over, crashing to the floor, as I scramble away from him.

Hades watches me, his eyes following my every move, as I try to put as much distance between us as possible. There's a predatory look on his face that I know far too well from my years spent avoiding my stepbrother's advances.

It unsettles me as he advances. It's clear that he will not simply allow me to leave, not when there's that hunger fueling his movements.

"No," I say, my voice coming out broken and shaky. "Please, no. I don't want this."

But of course, he ignores me as he throws my chair aside and closes the distance between us. A startled cry escapes me, my wrist caught all too easily in his hand. He pulls me roughly to him, bringing my body flush against his.

I scream out just as the double doors to the room crash open, and I look to see a massive wolf filling the hallway, flames licking up over its entire body as his eyes narrow on Hades and me.

HAZEL

Cerberus lets out a growl, sending chills cascading down my spine as he ducks to step into the room.

Every ounce of his humanity seems to have been lost, burned away in the fire that now encases him. His eyes flash and narrow as another low growl of warning escapes him.

Towering above me, Hades lets out a curse as his grip on my wrist tightens, taking out his frustration at Cerberus on me. Unable to stop myself, I let out a small whimper of pain as his fingers dig into my skin.

He glances down at me, surprise momentarily flickering across his face as he realizes that he's actually hurting me. He releases me, the concern instantly replaced by his usual stony expression.

I quickly step back, clutching my bruised wrist to my chest and wincing at the pain that gently radiates from it. Hades takes a step back as well, as if suddenly eager to put distance between us.

"We are finished here," he says. "Take her back to her room."

Cerberus lets out another growl, this time coming to stand between Hades and me. The flames slowly dying out as they flicker and dance around him, casting an eerie glow about the room.

For a moment, the two stare at each other, but then Cerberus quells the remaining fire with the shake of his fur coat. Turning toward me, he gently nudges me out of the room with his snout. I don't fight him on this, and find myself strangely comforted by his presence as we leave the private dining room behind.

It isn't until we're well away from Hades that he pauses to shift back into his human form.

Rage still rolls off of him as he stares at me. For a moment, I wonder if I've managed to do something to upset him.

As I meet his fiery gaze, questions rise up even through my wariness and confusion.

I thought he was supposed to be loyal to Hades ... and yet, he just saved me from the hands of the king.

His beloved master.

Surely, that goes against everything he stands for in this place.

I open my mouth, eager to have answers, but then I close it as he steps closer to me, his hands shaking with barely contained anger.

"Show me your wrist," he growls, his eyes ablaze from within.

I hesitate, only just now realizing I'm still clutching it to my chest, and slowly hold it out to him. He takes it tenderly in the heat of his own hand, turning it over as his jawline hardens.

"Does it hurt?"

"Only a little."

A low rumble rolls through him at this, and he releases my hand.

"Come, I must get you back to your room. Quickly."

Silence stretches between us as we continue the journey back to my tower. I chew my lip in ever-growing bewilderment as we start up the stairs that lead to my room.

Unable to help myself, my eyes continue to slip to him, but he refuses to look back or even acknowledge my presence again. I'm starting to get the sense that he wishes he hadn't interrupted Hades, and yet, I can't say that I'm upset that he did.

Questions flood my mind, dancing at the tip of my tongue as they beg to be asked. But I hold them at bay. In his current mood, I doubt I'll get any answers from him.

If he even has any answers to give.

We reach my room and I'm almost relieved to step over the threshold. At least here, I know the rules of the game, with no one but myself to entertain.

Cerberus' eyes scan the room before he nods to himself and turns to leave. I watch as his massive form bends to slip beneath the frame, and I suddenly realize that I still need to thank him.

He did, after all, save me from whatever it is Hades had planned for tonight.

"Cerberus, wait," I say, my voice coming out soft. He

pauses halfway out the door, his form strangely still for a moment. "Thank you. Truly."

I don't expect him to say anything back, let alone make it clear that he heard me, but then he slowly turns to meet my eyes over his shoulder. The fire in them is still smoldering, casting strange shadows across his face as he gives me a nod.

"You are welcome, mortal." Then, without another word, he closes the door and turns the key in the lock.

Alone again, I let out a sigh as I sink down onto the bed.

My entire body shudders as I draw in a breath and try to process everything that just happened between me and Hades. Though I'm not entirely sure what this shift in Hades actually means for me.

And then there's the question of Cerberus' loyalty.

Giving myself a moment to calm down, I stand and shake the confusion that's begun to cloud my head. I move into the bathroom, suddenly eager to wash away whatever remains of the sensation of his touch on my skin.

The hot water does little to ease my racing mind and heart, though. Even as I clean my face and change back into a simple nightgown, my thoughts keep returning to the events of the evening.

Somehow, I seem to have captured Hades' attention without even trying. Of course, it would be now that he took an interest in me. Now that I no longer want to step foot down that path.

I catch a glimpse of myself in the mirror.

Staring at my reflection, I can't help but wonder, why me?

What did I do to deserve this special place in hell?

All I wanted to do was to save my father's life.

And yet, somehow, I've not only failed at doing so, but I've also managed to end up in the Underworld as Hades' prisoner.

Too many questions bounce about my head. None of them with answers I can even pretend to grasp.

Shaking my head at my reflection, I leave the small bathroom and crawl into bed.

I need to talk to Persephone. The very next chance that I get, I need to tell her everything. I need to make her listen to me.

I should have done so last night; I realize that now and can only hope my hesitation doesn't prove to be disastrous for us both.

Tonight, I *will* find a way to talk to her. Otherwise, I fear I may not get another chance.

I just pray that she's willing to listen to what I have to say.

Sleep, of course, doesn't find me. It doesn't take long for me to give up on it, instead choosing to pace the room as I wait to be summoned to Persephone's nightly lessons.

The hours seem to drag on, time having no sympathy for me as I move to stare out of the window.

Finally, I hear the distant echo of footsteps traveling up the tower toward me.

The guards are finally coming to collect me.

I can't help the relief that washes over me at this. I had just begun to fear that something had happened and that there would be no lessons tonight.

That my chance to talk to Persephone was gone.

My relief is short-lived, though, as the footsteps stop well before they ever reach my door. Frowning, I move toward the door, impatience and worry overtaking me as I press an ear to the thick wood.

I can hear the low resonance of voices in the hall, but can't quite seem to make out what's being said. What I can make out though, is the deep rumble of Cerberus' voice as he argues with the guards come to fetch me.

It would appear that he didn't go very far when he left me earlier.

Dropping to my hands and knees, I hold my breath as I try to listen through the crack in the door.

"... no," comes Cerberus' deep voice.

No?

Surely, he must be aware of the nightly lessons the women have been attending with Persephone.

I close my eyes as I try to make out what the other guards say. It's hard to catch their every word, but it sounds like they are growing irate with him, and I manage to hear something that sounds like orders.

"She is to remain under my watch at all times. I care little for the orders you claim to have. Regardless of who gave them," Cerberus growls, his voice rising as it echoes off the walls. "I will not allow her to be swept away in the middle of the night."

The guards continue to argue with Cerberus, their

voices growing louder and more agitated, but I can already tell they're wasting their breath.

Cerberus will not relent. He's far too set on doing his duty as he stands guard over me. After what I witnessed at dinner, I'm not entirely certain he would even allow Hades to override his own overprotectiveness.

A cold sweat breaks out across my skin as panic rises within me, and I realize he's winning the argument. The other guards seem unwilling to go toe to toe with him, and I honestly can't blame them.

Even if I desperately need them to win.

I can't miss tonight's lesson; this may be my last chance to talk to Persephone and explain everything to her before it's too late.

I have to see her. Tonight.

As quiet falls in the hallway, I quickly push myself up off the floor and bring my fists to the door.

Cerberus might be able to intimidate the guards, but I will not allow him to do so to me. He can't ruin this for me, I simply won't allow it. Pounding my fists against the door as hard as I can, I wince at the pain that shoots up from my bruised wrist but don't allow it to hinder me.

"Guards!" I shout, hoping they can make out my words through the door. "I'm here, take me to Persephone!"

For one long moment, nothing happens, and fear that the guards can't hear me or that Cerberus will stop them fills my mind. I need to convince him that he must allow me to leave. I just need him to open the door.

"Cerberus, open this door," I demand as I continue to beat my fists against the door. I pause to listen, my breathing heavy before opening my mouth to repeat the command. But before I can say anything, I hear the approach of heavy footsteps.

I just barely manage to set my face as a key is shoved into the lock and the door swings open.

Cerberus glowers at me, looking just as displeased as I expected him to be, his massive frame filling the doorway and blocking my exit.

"I need to go," I inform him as he cocks his head at me. "Please, step aside."

"Out of the question."

"Please, Cerberus."

"No."

"I can't miss the lesson," I plead, clasping my hands together. "Please, I need to go."

"I said, no."

"You will only be putting me in more danger by refusing her."

His brow furrows at this. "How so?"

I fight back the smile that tugs at the corner of my lips as I realize that I may have found a way to convince him to let me go. He genuinely seems to care about keeping me safe, and right now I'm not above exploiting that ... not if it'll get me in front of Persephone.

"Persephone will suspect something has happened. She may even come after me herself, and then where would that leave us?"

"I can deal with Persephone."

"Or you can simply allow me to go and avoid the danger altogether."

"No."

"You can accompany me," I hasten to add. "You can do your duty while still appeasing the Queen's orders. Now, take me to the queen."

It almost seems too simple. A solution that will leave us both feeling as if we've won.

I'd be safe, under his watchful eye, and still have the chance to try to speak with Persephone.

He stares down at me, his head still cocked to one side as a glimmer of mischief flickers to life in his eyes ... and I know that I've won. Though he lets out a sigh, and his expression darkens as if preparing to tell me no again, I know he won't refuse.

"Very well," he finally concedes, "but if I see or hear *anything* that threatens your safety, anything odd or out of place, then I am dragging you right back here. I am not afraid to cause a scene either, if that is what it comes down to. Is that understood?"

"Yes," I answer.

He hesitates for another moment, continuing to block my path even though he's agreed to my terms.

I raise an eyebrow at him, unable to stop my nervous impatience at bay as it bubbles through me. We need to get moving if I want to make the lessons on time.

A few seconds go by, but then he nods and steps aside to let me out of the room. The other guards are still waiting on the stairs and appear more than a little relieved to see me.

Together, with Cerberus taking up the rear, they lead me through the palace.

The halls seem even more quiet than usual, and the only sounds to be heard are the echoes of our footsteps on the stone floor. Cerberus remains close behind me, his presence looming over me, like a shadow that refuses to let go ...

I'm more than a little surprised to find guards lining the corridor leading up to Persephone's jungle room. The two men with us join them as Cerberus takes the lead and pulls open the doors for me.

Stepping into the room, I'm more than a little relieved to be leaving the growing unease of the echoing hallways behind me, and I give him a small smile of thanks. I don't know why I expected him to wait in the hall with the others, but of course, he doesn't.

Cerberus hovers, following one step behind me as I move to join the other women.

We're late. Persephone is already standing in the midst of the room, her expression displeased as her eyes trail over Cerberus.

But she says nothing as I take my spot to one side. Tonight, I have even less hope of blending into the crowd. Not with Cerberus towering behind me, and the women around us stepping to the side, eager to put space between themselves and us.

"These lessons are for the women, only, Cerberus," Persephone finally says, making me cringe inwardly as the others look our way. "You are welcome; however, to wait *outside* with the other men."

"I will be staying."

"You—"

"I am to watch over the mortal, by Hades' orders," Cerberus says, cutting her off. "She is to remain within my sight at all times while outside her room."

Persephone's eyes narrow, her gaze flickering between Cerberus and me. I try to keep a neutral expression, not wanting to make the situation any more uncomfortable than it already is.

"Very well," she finally says, her expression hardening. "Then I suppose it only makes sense that you play the part of the mortal's partner."

I balk at this, my mouth going dry as I try and fail to get any words out.

"Fine," Cerberus snorts as if he's just been given a challenge he fully intends to win.

Persephone's smile doesn't quite meet her eyes as she nods in return before turning back to the others, ready to start the lesson.

I close my mouth as I try to swallow past my nerves, realizing that I get no say in any of this. I had hoped to once again find myself as Persephone's partner, but instead, she summons Lilia forward.

As I glance from her to Cerberus, I'm suddenly not so sure how I'm going to find the moment alone with Persephone that I so desperately need.

HAZEL

Persephone's eyes are cold as she glances about the room.

Though her gaze seems to easily move through Cerberus, I can't help but notice the small pause as she turns back to the redhead at her side.

"Tonight, we will focus on the more ... *intimate* details when it comes to pleasing Hades," she tells us.

As she begins the lesson, I wonder if this is some way of her getting back at Cerberus, and in a way Hades for assigning him to me.

My cheeks redden as I do my best to pay attention to her lesson. Yet, I barely register a word she says as she intimately wraps herself around her new partner and sets about explaining her movements in graphic detail.

"Now, it is your turn," she says, her smile finally managing to break the ice in her gaze as she flashes a look at the hellhound.

Slowly, I turn to face Cerberus. I'm already burning with embarrassment at the mere thought of practicing any of these movements with him. My mind spins as I try to figure out a way to get out of this.

Perhaps it was a mistake to convince him to bring me here.

I need to speak with Persephone, but at this point, I'm not sure that will even be possible.

"Do wish me to start?" Cerberus asks, drawing my attention back to him.

I nod absentmindedly, and he steps closer.

"Stay where you are," Persephone says. "Allow the girl to practice on you, not the other way around."

Swallowing hard, I try to focus on the task at hand. I move closer to him, reluctantly reaching out to place my palm against his hard chest. Slowly, I circle him, tracing the lines of his body as I draw nearer with each step. By the time I return to face him, our bodies are barely an inch apart.

Cerberus looks down at me, his eyes darkening with an intensity that sends shivers down my spine. I can feel the heat radiating off his body, and my skin prickles with anticipation. My heart pounds in my ears as I try my best to ignore these sensations and quickly refocus on the lesson at hand.

"Now, Hazel," Persephone says, her voice low and sultry. "I want you to show me what you have learned."

I take a deep breath to steady myself before moving closer to Cerberus. I can feel his muscles tense beneath my touch, and I have to fight the urge to pull away even as he shifts slightly closer.

His body brushes against mine, our eyes meet, and I watch the fire in his gaze roar to life, the flames burning bright blue. Then his hands reach for my hips, pulling even closer to him so that I can feel every inch of him pressed against me.

"Remember what I showed you," Persephone calls out.

Blinking, I run my hands up his chest, letting one come to rest there as I rise onto the tips of my toes and run my fingers through his hair.

His dark hair is as soft and thick as his fur looked when I first met him. As I reach the back of his head, I grab a handful of it and gently tug to bring his face down to mine.

We're mere inches apart now, our breaths becoming one, as our eyes meet once more. The fire within him licks at the edges of his eyes as he stares at me, and my breath catches in my throat as he leans forward so that there's but a hair's width between our lips.

Then, he bursts into flames.

I cry out in shock and pain as flames lick up around me. Stumbling from his arms, I hurry to pat myself down before collapsing to the ground to catch my breath.

Cerberus' eyes are wide as he stares down at me in stunned silence.

"Did I hurt you?" he asks as soon as he finds his voice.

I glance down at myself, half-expecting to find that my nightgown caught fire. But other than a few snaking vines of red where the fire touched my skin, I'm unharmed.

If a bit sooty.

"Hazel?" Persephone is at my side before I can answer

Cerberus, concern on her brow as her eyes trail over me. "Are you alright?"

I give her a dazed nod but flinch as one of the burn marks starts to smart.

"Here, come with me," she says, helping me to my feet. "Everyone else, continue practicing! And you, out, now! You are putting her and the rest of us in danger with your very presence."

Cerberus looks uncertain but then excuses himself as his eyes trail over the burns on my arms. Still, I can't help but watch his retreat, caught between worry and fear.

"Hazel?" I blink several times before turning back to Persephone. The sweet smell of fresh flowers wafts over me, her expression far softer now that Cerberus has stepped out of the room.

It only takes me a second to realize the opportunity I've just been given.

"I need to speak with you," I whisper.

Persephone glances around at the others before nodding. "This way."

Wrapping an arm around my waist, she leads me to the back of the room. Under the pretense of tending to me, she settles me onto a lounge made entirely of vines and flowers and bustles about me. Her hands are warm as she wraps large, bright yellow blossoms around my arms.

"To heal the skin," she tells me.

I smile, working up the courage to tell her what I need to. This is my chance and I would be a fool to let it pass me by.

My mouth opens, but no words come out.

"Now, what is it you wish to tell me?"

As if this was all I needed to hear, my tongue loosens and words begin to spill from me. I tell her everything, no detail too small, about the ball, my plans, and the dinner I just had with Hades.

She watches me, her fingers stiffening on me as I finally tell her about Hades' kiss. Around us, the temperature in the room begins to dip, and the plants and flowers shrivel as her eyes lift to meet mine.

"It was you."

"What?" I gasp, flinching at the quiet venom in her voice.

"You are the one he plans to replace me with, and you knew it."

I blink, my mouth opening but no words come out as her fingers wrap around my wrists. Her grip is tight as she stares up at me, an iciness like I've never seen before fills her eyes as she leans closer.

"And you kept this from me. All this time, I thought you were my friend ... but you have been trying to steal my husband behind my back."

"No," I quickly say. "Persephone, please."

"I should have known. Oh, what a fool I have been. Of course, it had to be you. After what he did to bring me here ..." she trails off at this, pain flickering across her face before it's quickly replaced with rage.

"No, you must believe me," I plead. "I have no desire to take your place, let alone steal your husband. I only wanted to save my life and that of my father."

"Lies."

"Please, Persephone."

"Why should I believe you?" she demands.

I pause, my heart pounding in my chest as I think of an answer to give her, before whispering, "Because my heart belongs to another."

Persephone pulls back slightly at this. Her eyes search my face and for a moment I think I've finally managed to get through to her.

"Who?"

"I-I—"

"Give me a name, mortal."

I blink at her, suddenly not sure how to answer her question. Death had seemed wary of letting these gods know about his feelings for me. Perhaps there is a reason he didn't want them to know.

Would she even believe it possible that I still love Death, despite his betrayal? Or would it be safer to claim that Eros or some other man has won me over?

Does it even matter who it is as long as I give her a name other than Hades?

I *do* care for Eros, but I know it would be a lie to say that I was in love with him.

Not when it is Death who still holds my heart captive.

Death whom I still long for, and whose touch I crave in the darkest hours of night.

And yet, it isn't his name that falls from my lips.

"Eros," I tell her.

23

HAZEL

"You *lie*," Persephone hisses, thorns springing up around her as her voice rings out through the room.

I do my best to keep a straight face, forcing myself not to wince even as the other women shrink back into the shadows, startled by the sudden change in atmosphere.

Guilt has already pitted in my stomach, the lie bitter on my tongue. But it's too late to take back Eros' name without making the situation even worse for us both.

All she really needs to believe is that I have feelings for someone, anyone, other than Hades. As much as it sickens me to do so, I need to sell this lie to her.

"You don't have to believe me," I tell her, barely able to hear myself over the pounding of my heart in my ears. "You can see for yourself."

"What do you mean?"

"Hades had Eros imprisoned earlier today for trying to help me to escape."

Persephone's eyes narrow as she stares at me for a long moment. Then, she rises without a word.

Crossing the room, I watch her open the doors and speak with several of her guards. The other women glance nervously at each other as she re-enters the room, closing the doors behind her.

"We shall see," she says as she returns to stand nearby.

The seconds seem to pass all too slowly as the room around us grows still. An icy chill rolls off of Persephone, her arms crossed over her chest and her gaze locked on the double doors.

I do my best to remain motionless where I am, worried that any movement might cause her to unleash her anger on me.

After what feels like an eternity, the doors finally open and two massive guards step into the room, dragging Eros between them. I can't help the gasp that escapes me as I take in the gag in Eros's mouth and the chains around his wrists and ankles.

"It would appear that you were telling the truth," Persephone says, her eyes moving over Eros who is being all but dragged toward us.

My heart aches as I find my own gaze fixed on the pale god. He still looks as beautiful as ever, though the grime of the dungeons seems to cling to nearly every inch of him, and his long white hair hangs down around him in a tangled mess.

It's clear that he's been tortured.

Fresh blood has yet to dry as it mixes with the dirt that stains his usually pristinely-white clothing. Bruises have blossomed into horrid patches of blue and purple across his otherwise colorless face.

"Come," she says. "Bring him over here."

Leading the guards and Eros, Persephone motions toward me.

They stop before me, the guards forcing Eros to his knees, and he lets out a sound that wounds me as his face twists in pain.

"Eros," I breathe, and in an instant his white eyes are on me, his own agony momentarily forgotten.

"Mortal ... are you okay?" he asks, but my answer is cut off by Persephone moving between us, her gaze settling on me with a challenge in her eyes.

"Prove it," she says, her tone flat and emotionless.

"Prove what?" I ask

"That you are in love with him."

Eros looks as confused as I feel, his brow furrowing as his eyes shift between us. I don't know what to say or do that would be enough to convince her that I love him.

"How can I prove it to you?" I ask, looking up at her.

"Lie with him."

My heart stops at her words, my mind racing as I try to come up with a way out of this.

"Here?"

"Yes."

With a wave of her hand, a beautiful bed of intertwined branches and thick moss rises from the floor, curtained by hanging vines covered in tiny white flowers. I suppose I should be grateful that she's offering some privacy to us, but that does nothing to stop the heat that rises within my cheeks.

"I-I can't," I stutter, shaking my head. "Not here."

"Then you are lying," Persephone states, her voice sharp. "Guards, seize her, and return Eros to the dungeons."

"Wait," I cry out, and she holds up a hand to her men.

"Well," she prompts as I remain frozen.

"I'll do it."

She signals to the guards to free Eros from his shackles.

Hesitantly, I rise and move toward him, reaching out to offer him my hand. He takes it, his hand uncharacteristically cold as it slips into mine, and I instantly feel the pull of energy as it seeps out of me and into him.

Eros grimaces as he gets to his feet and allows me to lead him over to the bed of moss and vines. It *almost* looks welcoming as I shift the curtain of flowers out of the way. I sit down on the bed and gently pull Eros down next to me, my heart pounding so hard that I swear I can feel it in my throat.

Turning toward Eros, I study his face, taking in the pain and torture now etched into his features. Bruises and cuts mar his otherwise perfect skin, and my heart breaks at the thought of what he has endured for my sake.

That he has been tortured because of *me*.

I reach up to tenderly cup his cheek in my hand, before leaning in to press a gentle kiss to his lips. Eros responds, his lips moving against mine as his arms wrap around me, pulling me closer.

He deepens our kiss, and I try my best to give in to the moment as I move to straddle his lap. His own hand cupping my face as the other roams lower over my body, tracing every curve as if he's desperate to memorize me.

My own hands slip lower, and I can feel his arousal growing beneath me as my own urgency builds. Desperation starts to rise within me as my heart wars with my body, reminders of Death flickering through my mind with ever-increasing frequency.

Suddenly, Eros stills at my touch.

Breaking our kiss, he pulls back, his eyes filled with a mixture of desire and pain, and I can feel the weight of Persephone's gaze on us.

"I cannot do this," he says, lifting me off of him as he rises from the bed.

"What?" I ask, confused.

"I can hardly believe I am saying this, but I cannot claim you when your heart still so clearly cries out for another," Eros says, with a sharp snort. "You love him, mortal, no matter how much you try to deny it. I can feel nothing but your desire for him ... and I will not take you when it is not *me* that you want."

His words hit me like a punch to the gut, and I can feel tears prickling at the corners of my eyes.

"Eros ..." I murmur, my voice barely more than a whisper as he reaches for the vines.

He pauses as he glances back at me, his face filled with a mixture of pain and sorrow.

"Mortal," he says, his voice suddenly so soft that I can barely hear him. "What I am trying to say is that ... I love you."

I open my mouth to reply, but before I can say anything, there's a heavy thud and Eros' eyes roll back in his head. I let out a startled scream as I watch Eros collapse to the floor, a guard standing just beyond the curtain of vines.

I watch in stunned horror for a moment as another guard steps up to help him drag Eros from the room.

"Wait, no! Stop," I cry as I scramble from the bed, but my words fall on deaf ears.

The guards don't so much as glance back at me as they drag the god's unconscious form past Persephone and the other women.

Tears stream down my cheeks as worry fills me, and I almost don't see Persephone turning to stare at me. Pain and rage flash within her gaze as she moves closer. Betrayal making her features sharp.

"Guards, remove her from my presence, at once," she demands.

Quickly trying to overcome the stunned shock that hits me, I realize what's happening.

Persephone is already moving away from me, though, as her guards step in to obey her orders.

"No, Persephone, please."

But she doesn't so much as turn to look back at me.

"I am sorry. I should have told you," I tell her, my voice catching on to the last word.

"Silence, *mortal*."

I flinch at the way she spits out the word, as if what I am now disgusts her. It doesn't matter that Eros was talking about my love for Death, not her husband, Hades.

It doesn't matter that she couldn't hear him tell me that he loves me.

I have only proven myself a liar to her, and she has no reason to believe me.

"Persephone," I try once more, but the rest of my words are trapped within my mouth as a series of vines snake up my body; one wrapping tightly around my head, effectively silencing me.

Tears stream down my face as the guards grab my arms, and. Persephone doesn't so much as a glance in my direction as I'm taken from the room.

No sooner than the doors have closed behind us than another voice demands the men carrying me to stop. My heart pounds in my chest as Deimos steps into view.

"Where are you taking her?"

"The dungeons."

"For what reason? Has Hades order this?"

"No, my lord," one of the guards answers hesitantly. "The queen—"

"Hand her over, the king has final say over what happens to these women." The men hesitate for a second, and Deimos' face darkens. "That was an order! Hand her over at once! She is to be brought before the king."

The next thing I know, Deimos' hand wraps around me, and I'm being hurried through the palace ... toward Hades.

24

EROS

I wake to the throbbing of my head. Fingers dig painfully into my arms, and it takes me a moment to realize that I am being dragged down a hallway.

For one moment, I consider putting up a fight, but then I hear the rattle of chains against the floor. They must have re-shackled my hands and feet after leaving Persephone's little training grounds.

I let out a groan as they drag me roughly down a flight of stairs, alerting them to my growing awareness and their hands tighten on my arms.

"Let me go," I command, grateful they at least forgot to gag me.

Of course, the guards ignore me.

They ignore my words. Struggling against their grips only makes their grips tighten, deepening the bruising that already covers my arms.

Not that they care. I am not the god they serve.

Still, I find annoyance building steadily within me as I

am once more dragged down, down, down into Hade's cold dungeon.

I am tossed unceremoniously into a cell, where I land in a heap, the very air knocked out of me.

I do not move for several moments, letting my breath come back as I try to sort my thoughts. I need to come up with a way to save Hazel. Things are far more dire than even I realized.

Again, this is all my fault.

I should have known better than to play around with the forces of love. Obviously, I have proven to be a poor guardian of it.

As much as I wanted to give in to the mortal's touch, I could not. I have never felt the love that Hazel feels for Death until tonight, and it broke me that even when touching me, she desired *him*.

My brother and I have had our differences when it comes to love and lust, but even I will not bed a woman who does not wish me to.

Anteros.

Sitting up slowly, I realize that I have a plan, or at least something that could loosely be called that. Death would most certainly disagree, but he is not here.

I am.

And right now, this may be the only way to save Hazel from this mess with Hades. The only way to get word to Death about what is going on.

Though it will not be easy, this could even be the answer to *all* our problems.

I am almost gleeful as I drag myself to my feet. Quieting myself, I close my eyes to listen and am made distantly aware of a guard's approaching footsteps as he makes his rounds.

I wait, trying to be patient.

When the guard finally makes his slow approach, I pull myself closer to the cold metal bars of the cell. He pauses several cells down, sneering at whatever unfortunate soul has found themselves there before continuing on toward me.

I do my best to school the crooked grin on my face. I cannot have him suspecting what I am up to.

"Move back," the guard snaps, kicking the door of my cell with a heavy boot.

"I do not think I will."

"Do not make me come in there," the guard says. "I would be more than happy to teach you a thing or two about respect."

I cannot stop myself from snorting at this. Does he not see how far torture has gotten anyone else with me?

"I would like an audience with Hades. Tell him his guest, Eros, is requesting it."

The guard laughs at this before continuing on, ignoring my request.

I wait until he makes it several cells down before I call out to him again, repeating my request. He ignores me but that only encourages me to shout loudly.

With his hand on the door, about to leave the cells behind to enter the guards' quarters, I smile.

"Fine, then I call upon the God of Love," I shout. "I call upon my brother, Anteros, for a Trial of Love."

Frozen for a moment, I can hear the guard's boots slowly scraping against the dirty floor as he turns toward me. I can feel his agitation like static through the air, stress and worry mixing with it.

"What did you say?"

Sighing, I repeat, "I call upon Anteros. I demand a Trial of Love."

There is a long pause as the guard stares at me.

"Do you understand the consequences of invoking such a thing?" the guard snarls, storming closer as if to intimidate me.

"Obviously," I scoff. "He is my brother after all."

The guard hesitates, clearly unsure how to handle this.

I am sure that in all his years spent serving Hades, he has never had to deal with something like this.

"To hell with you, Eros," the guard spits, finally turning to leave. I cannot help but smile at the reluctance in his steps as he goes to relay my request.

I cannot almost imagine Hades' expression when he learns what I have asked for. Hopefully, this will be just what we need to outsmart him at his own game.

Of course, Anteros will be none too thrilled to be summoned away from his wife, especially to such a place as this.

Alone in the cell, the weight of what I have just done begins to grow heavy as I consider everything it may entail. I know it is dangerous to involve my brother. Perhaps even foolish, but I cannot think of any other way to help the mortal.

She cannot be allowed to remain here. Not when it is clear that something even more sinister is at play.

I am not about to let Hades get away with using her as

some pawn in his fight for power. Or as just another plaything to be tossed aside once he has satisfied himself with her.

This thought in particular has me pacing my cell, though it is not easy given the chains.

This is my only choice.

Anteros and Hades be damned. I do not want to do this, but what other way is there?

This may be the only way we can rescue the mortal alive.

These thoughts keep spinning in my head as I pace, waiting. After what feels like several thousand eternities, I finally hear the sound of returning footsteps.

My own pacing stops as I make out the all-too-familiar steps of my brother's gait. Already his annoyance clear in his muttered curses as he is led to my cell.

I flinch at the squeal of the door before the dungeon hallway fills with guards and then my brother. Fury swirls around him as he lets out a sharp exhale and stops before me.

Obviously, he is less than thrilled to have been summoned away from his honeymoon to deal with me.

"What is it now, Eros?"

"I have summoned you, dear brother," I say with a smile. "To carry out a Trial of Love."

"You jest," he says, stepping closer to the bars that separate us. "You hate love."

"I do not *hate* it," I answer carefully. "I simply have never understood it, until now. I have summoned you, because I believe a Trial of Love is the only way to save the fate of someone I know. Someone I care deeply for."

He shifts closer, doubt heavy in his presence. "What kind of game are you playing at, Eros?"

"It is not about me."

My brother lets out a humorless laugh at this, his disbelief now only outweighed by his annoyance. I wait, hoping that his curiosity will get the better of him if I do not react ... and if his curiosity fails, I hope his sense of duty will not.

"Not about you?" he asks. "What in the Underworld are you talking about? I have never known anything to *not* be about you. I was not aware you were even conscious of anyone outside yourself."

Clearly, he is not convinced. I am more than a little irked by this, but I cannot say that I am surprised. He is not *entirely* wrong about my previous disregard for most everyone and everything.

But I cannot allow him to waste any more of what little time we have.

"It does not matter much your opinions here, dearest brother. I will continue to stand here, demanding that you carry out a Trial of Love, until you do exactly that."

"You are being serious?"

"Yes."

"I must remind you, Eros," my brother says, his tone suddenly very solemn, "of the consequences of calling for such a trial."

"I am *well* aware."

"If you do this and you are wrong, it will only result in slow torment and eventual death."

I let out a pained groan of frustration.

"Yes. I am aware, and I understand. Now, can we

hurry up and move this along? I am sure we both have things we would like to get back to."

"Fine," my brother says through gritted teeth, "and who is it, exactly, that is to be put on trial?"

"A mortal," I reply.

"And this mortal's name?"

"Her name is Hazel."

25

HAZEL

Deimos is silent at my side as he guides me through the palace.

Trailing behind us are several of Hades' stone guards, as if making sure no one gets in our way to stop me from being taken to the king.

"Where is she? Where is the mortal?!" My heart leaps at the sound of Cerberus' voice ringing out as it echoes distantly through the halls behind me.

Deimos' nostrils flare at this, his grip only tightening on me as he quickens our pace. I peek up at him, feeling the tension that rolls off him in heavy waves. I glance back, but my heart sinks as I am unable to spot Cerberus past the stone guards as we hurry through the halls.

"Pick up your feet," Deimos hisses as we reach a wing of the palace that I don't believe I've seen before. It seems darker than the rest, even the air feels heavier here.

We finally come to a stop in front of a towering set of ornate black doors. I don't need to feel the way Deimos straightens beside me to know what must lie beyond those doors.

He opens his mouth as if to say something, but then he closes it. Stepping forward to push open the doors, Deimos all but throws me inside the room beyond.

I stumble, but manage to catch myself before I can crash to the floor. Spinning around, I race toward the doors, but I'm too slow as they slam in my face.

And a key turns in the lock, trapping me alone inside the room.

Alone but for Hades, somewhere deeper in the depths of darkness.

The vines that were covering my mouth turn to dust, and I have to pinch my nose to keep from sneezing in surprise. Slowly, I turn to face the room, doing my best to make as little sound as possible as I press my back against the doors.

My eyes take a long moment to adjust to the dark, but even as they do, I can still barely make anything out. Vague silhouettes seem to rise all around me, taking on new shapes in my imagination with each blink of my eyes.

Swallowing, I turn back to the doors. It takes me a moment to feel out the handle, but no matter how I pull at them, they refuse to budge.

"Who goes there?" comes a deep rolling voice, cutting through the night air.

My heart leaps into my throat, my body tense as I turn back to face the room. Chills dance over my skin, a cold sweat breaking out across my forehead and chest. Taking a quiet breath in, I force myself to hold my head high as I stare into the unending void before me.

Blood pounds in my ears as my eyes, trail over the room. I can just barely make out the soft rustling of fabric moving about the room, but I cannot tell where it is coming from.

Then, the shadows take shape, and a massive form appears just before me. I flatten myself against the door as the spicy musk of Hades' scent washes around me, prickling at the back of my throat and nose. Slowly lifting my eyes, I peer up at him through my lashes as he looms up above me like the true nightmare that he is.

"Ah, if it is not the mortal herself."

His deep voice sends chills dripping down my spine as he reaches out a hand to caress my face. It takes everything in me not to grimace at his touch.

His fingers run over my cheeks before they stop at my chin, pinching it he tilts my face up until I have no choice but to look him in the eye. Bright sapphire flames burst to life around his head and shoulders, before smoldering into a soft blue glow that illuminates the rest of his skin with the same eerie hue.

"What are you doing here?"

I swallow past the lump quickly forming in my throat, and he takes my moment of silence to lean down, his free hand coming to cage me in as it rests on the door behind me. The entire lower half of his body presses against mine, pinning me to the door as his gaze drops to my lips.

It's only as he starts to bend to press his lips to mine in a kiss that I finally find my voice.

"I was with Persephone, your wife," I tell him. "I-I just told her about us."

A hiss slips through his lips at this, but it's enough to have him stepping back from me.

"I told you not to mention her in my presence," he snarls at me. "I thought I made myself very clear about this."

His eyes blaze with an infernal fury, and I can feel the heat of his power radiating off him like a furnace.

For a moment, I fear that he might strike me down where I stand. But instead, he turns and disappears into the darkness, though I can now make out his angry steps as he storms about the room.

A soft blue glow outlines his broad frame, and I can just make out the shape of him as he paces back and forth. He stops at a table and I have to squint to make him out as he pours himself a glass of wine.

His eyes snap up, cold dread filling me as he easily meets my gaze.

Downing the goblet of wine, he snaps his fingers and several candles flicker to life, casting blue light around the room. It's only now that I realize he's only wearing a pair of black silk pants, his powerful chest exposed by the flickering of the candles.

He is beautiful and terrifying in the way only a god can be, strength chiseling every line of his body in sharp angles.

He stays where he is, watching me from across the room. There is something uncertain in the way he looks at me that gives me a small rush of courage, and I take a tentative step away from the door and further into the room.

I can only hope that the mention of his wife is enough to have turned him off of wanting me. That he won't try anything else with her name hanging between us.

I'm not sure I understand his reaction to me mentioning her, but if it keeps him away from me, then I'm not willing to question it.

"Persephone has been teaching us how to seduce you," I say, my voice shaky as I once again disobey his orders, "but you should know that I have no desire to do so."

He neither reacts nor says anything in response to this.

Instead, Hades simply pours himself another glass of wine. Emboldened, I search for the right words to explain my behavior here and at the ball. Telling him the same thing I told Persephone not that long ago.

He tenses as I talk, but makes no attempt to stop me from speaking. As I finish, silence once again fills the room.

Hades doesn't meet my gaze this time as he pours another glass of wine ... then yet another, each downed in a single mouthful.

I take another step forward, knowing that I'm treading on thin ice. He turns so that his back is to me as I wait for some response to what I've just told him. His lack of a reaction gives me the courage to move even closer so that all that stands between us is the table.

"She loves you, even if you do no—"

He whirls on me at this, reaching across the table to

grab my bruised wrist, his crystal goblet shattering at his feet. A cry of pain escapes me as his hand tightens around me, his gaze burning with terrifying intensity.

Twisting my arm, he drags me forward over the table, knocking the decanter to the floor with a crash. A cry of pain slips from my lips as I struggle to alleviate the pain from his grip, but it only grows worse with each movement.

Pulling me closer to him, he towers over me where I lie on the table.

"I told you not to speak of my wife," he says, his voice so sharp that I wish he'd shouted instead.

With that, he jerks me off the table, tossing me to the ground where I land amongst the shattered crystal with a shriek of agony. Hot searing pain overtakes me as blood and tears mix.

I stare up at him, gasping for breath as I try to scramble off the glass, but my movements only make things worse. Hades reaches for me, his hand wrapping around my throat as he presses me back down against the floor.

New shards bite into my skin as my lungs constrict, burning with their need for air. My vision darkens for a moment, the room once more cast into impossible blackness.

Vaguely, I'm made aware of a commotion followed by the howling of a beast outside the room before Hades releases his hold on my throat. I choke as I suck in air, filling my lungs as best I can.

Hades strides across the room. Then a thundering

sound crashes through the night, making me wince, as a heavy bar is secured into place across the doors.

I can hear the sound of claws dragging across the wood from outside, but to no avail.

I am imprisoned here.

Without any hope of rescue from Hades' wrath.

26

CERBERUS

Panic and desperation fill me as I do my best to tear the damn doors off their hinges.

I am consumed by my need to get to the mortal.

Hades is meant to hold all my loyalties, without question or hesitation. Yet, all I can think about is saving her.

Of protecting her from *him*.

But no matter how much anger I throw into my attacks, the doors do not so much as budge. Then I remember the deal.

I quickly realize that I will not be able to accomplish this on my own.

Hades asinine deal with the Fates makes it impossible for me to step foot in his personal chambers.

Reluctantly, I step away from the door, crushing Deimos' leg beneath my foot in the process. Not that it matters now.

The silence that comes from within does not sit well with me.

Turning, I race away from Hades' chambers as fast as my legs will carry me through the palace hallways and out into the city.

Lifting my nose, I lock on to the scent I am searching for and tear after it.

Death is her only hope of surviving the night.

I am nearly gasping for air by the time I finally find the man himself just outside the city gates. As expected, dark shadows power and worry swirl about him as he strides toward me.

"Cerberus," Death says, his voice cold as I shift back to my human form and his eyes snap to mine.

"The mortal," I gasp, sucking in air. "Where have you been?"

"I was looking for Hazel's brother. What has happened?" he immediately demands. "Where is she?"

I am unable to answer as my lungs strain, the shift back to my human form taking its toll on me.

Death steps forward, a gloved hand taking a handful of my shirt as he drags me up to his height.

Our eyes meet, and I finally see the same fire burning in him that has awoken in me. See the same desperate need to protect her above all else.

Whatever the cost.

"Answer the question, now!"

Swallowing, I tell him what has happened. His grip on me tightens as he listens.

As soon as I mention Hades' bedchambers, he lets out a swear. Tossing me aside, he storms past me.

"You had better hope that we are not too late," he

snarls. "Or there will be hell to pay for every last being in this damned realm."

I scramble to my feet and race after him.

Little does Death know that he is not the only one who will help raze the Underworld to the ground if we are too late to save the mortal.

Reaching Hades' palace, two stone guards move to block our entry, but they stand no chance against Death.

I watch in stunned silence as Death's shadows burst out from him, covering the stone giants in darkness so cold they crack and then explode into a thousand frozen shards. We crash through the main doors just as several of Deimos' guards round the corner, drawn by the sound of the explosion.

Death waves a hand, his shadows rushing to fill the hall and shred through the men as he storms forward.

"The Fates' deal," I shout after him, but Death doesn't pay me any mind as he cuts his way through anyone who dares to stand in his way.

Shit.

Watching after him, I consider my options for a moment before splitting off in another direction. Instead of returning to Hades' rooms, I head toward the dungeon.

At this rate, we are going to need all the help we can get.

27

HAZEL

As I lay on the ground, gasping for air, rage pours from Hades in heavy waves as he paces the room yet again.

I can feel blood seeping down my arm from the cuts the crystal has made, and my throat aches from Hades' grip. I try to push myself up, but the pain in my ribs and the cuts on my skin make it nearly impossible as I let out a small whimper.

Another mistake.

His eyes flicker to me, and unable to stop himself, he bursts into blue flames. Despite the glass scattered on the ground, I do my best to scramble further away from the flames and the man as he takes a step toward me.

He lets out a low growl of anger as he reaches for me, his fingers just grazing my arm before I'm out of his reach. Pain makes my movements slow as I climb to my feet, swaying on my legs. He moves toward me again and I dodge him as I hurry to put more space between us, nearly tripping over myself in the process.

Again, his snarl fills the air as I do my best to keep my distance.

My eyes dart toward the door but the claws have long since fallen quiet. I am alone in here, the door locked, and Death none the wiser to my current plight.

I have no hope of anyone being able to get to me.

I've been such a fool.

Swallowing my dread, I reach for courage. I haven't come this far to just give up now, or let Hades end me like this.

Not without a fight.

My steps are shaky as I do my best to keep a wide berth between myself and the bright blue flames that are Hades. He continues to stalk toward me though, almost seeming to enjoy the chase.

After all, in the end, there's nowhere for me to go. I'm trapped here with him, and each time he lunges and misses, I feel the tension between us grow. Minutes begin to slip by, and I'm starting to wonder just how long I can keep this up.

The blood has started to dry on my skin, caking it, and I wince as I glance at the shards of glass that still protrude from my arms.

"Please," I gasp. "Spare me, please."

Hades lets out a low snort at this.

He's obviously not interested in my pleas let alone offering me mercy as he stalks closer, once more nearly catching me as I barely manage to slip through his fingers. Exhaustion and terror are weighing heavily on me as I move.

Again, I fear that I can't keep this up for much longer.

After several more attempts to catch me, Hades lets out a growl before stalking away from me. For a moment, relief floods me. Until he turns to look at me with a wicked grin on his face, his blue flames flickering dangerously around him.

"You are a fighter, I will give you that," he says, circling me like a predator as he reaches for something just out of my line of sight. "But you should have known better than to cross me."

I don't see what he grabs until he pulls a helmet over his head, and suddenly vanishes into thin air ... plunging me into darkness as all the candles flicker out.

Horror slices through me as my gaze jumps about the room, but the blue flames that alerted me to his movements are now gone. I have no idea where he's gone.

My heart thunders in my ears as I take several steps back, desperately trying to guess where he might be. I try to quiet my breathing in an effort to listen for footsteps, but it's impossible to hear anything besides the pounding of my own heart.

Then I feel the heat of his breath on the back of my neck as invisible fingers wrap around my shoulder.

I shriek, turning out of his grip as I stumble backward, tripping over my own feet in the process. Landing hard on the floor, my eyes widen as Hades appears directly above me. His feet planted on either side of me, he tosses the helmet to one side as he stares down at me with a wicked grin.

"Please," I gasp shaking my head.

His lip curls up in a sneer as he reaches for me, his

fingers cutting into my arms as they push several shards of glass that much deeper into my skin. Hades pulls me to my feet, unbothered by the way I wince and gasp in pain from his touch.

Fear grips my heart as he drags me across the room and toward his massive bed, covered in dark silk sheets.

"Silence, mortal," he hisses. "You must pay for your disobedience."

With that, he tosses me onto the silk sheets.

My body trembles as he climbs onto the bed beside me, his cold blue eyes searching my face as he secures me beneath him.

I'm pinned in place as his hands move along my curves, forcing his way between my legs. I can't move, can't speak as he stares down at me with a cocky grin, and I know that this is it.

This is the end.

But then fight fills my body.

I will not allow him to just take me.

Thrashing about, I try to escape his grip. Bucking my hips against him does nothing to shift his weight off of me, but it is enough to frustrate him. After a moment, his hands reach for my wrists to jerk them up over my head, further pinning me to the bed.

Still, I don't let this stop me from continuing my fight. If he thinks I will make this easy, then he has another thing coming.

Tears sting my eyes as he moves my wrists together, freeing one hand to run down over my body. Grabbing the neckline of my nightgown, he tears it open to expose my breasts to him, and I still continue to twist away from him as I best can.

He growls in frustration that I've yet to submit to him.

His anger only seems to grow now the more I fight him, but he refuses to give up. His hand slips to my waist, where he grabs a hand full of my dress and yanks it further up.

I thrash as much as I can, not that it does me any good. He still moves my skirts out of the way all too easily.

"No," I gasp as his hand slips between my thighs.

His lips pull into a triumphant grin as he shifts atop me, just enough for him to remove himself from his pants. I try to use the moment to gain some freedom, but it's not enough as he releases my wrists to close his hand over my throat, choking me even as his weight returns to my body all too soon.

I claw at his hand as I struggle to breathe, but even I know what comes next.

Cold dread pools in my stomach as he moves to adjust himself and I brace for what he's about to take from me.

But before he can steal what he wants from me, the doors to the room explode into a thousand pieces.

Shrapnel rains down on us, most of it pelting Hades as it burrows its way into his skin. He lets out a roar of rage and pain as he turns to see who's come to interrupt us.

Taking the opportunity to scramble a few inches back, I glance around him to see the figure framed in the gaping hole where the doors once were.

Standing there with inky black shadows surging up around him is Death.

My Death.

28

DEATH

A fury unlike anything I have ever known rises within me at the sight before me.

Power and rage course through my veins, mixing with the very essence of my being. I want nothing more than this man's death.

Striding further into the room I feel the power pouring from me, feeding the shadows that swirl around me. My form grows with each step, the dark power within me growing more set on vengeance and bloodshed by the second.

"Hades," I say, my voice booming through the room. "Release her to me."

"Or what?" Hades questions. "You forget yourself, Death. This is my kingdom, and she does not leave without my permission."

He sounds more than a little irate as he removes himself from the bed and Hazel. Standing in what I think he means to be intimidating, I have to fight back a laugh.

He is *nothing* compared to me. His powers are limited

but not mine. Death, it seems, outweighs all else, even in his own kingdom.

My eyes glance over his shoulder as Hazel curls up on the bed, tugging at her nightgown as she grimaces in pain. The way her body quivers shatters my heart as I fear I came too late.

That Hades has already broken yet another mortal woman with his greed.

My anger swells as I turn my gaze back to him.

"You will pay for what you have done to her," I roar.

"Do your worst," Hades snorts at this and Hazel flinches slightly. "Let me taste of your powers."

I pause at this, but then Hazel shifts and I catch sight of the blood caked on her soft skin. The sight stops my heart for a moment.

She is injured, bleeding in his bed as she cowers from whatever nightmare he put her through.

I will kill him.

Unable to stop myself, I launch at him.

He meets me midway with fists that do not meet their mark. My strength is too great, too fierce for him to stop me. My rage fueling each and every blow I land.

Power be damned, I would rather kill him with my bare hands anyway.

The gods may be powerful, but I am Death, and I will not be stopped.

Still, Hades matches my hits, landing a few good punches of his own as we tear into each other with every ounce of power we have in us.

It feels good to finally drive my fists into him. His

sputtering sounds almost bring a grin to my face ... *almost*.

He still deserves so much worse for all the wrongs he has committed.

Hades puts up a tough fight but eventually, I manage to get the upper hand.

Lifting him from the ground by his neck, his eyes widen for a moment as he finally realizes just how powerless he is. I cannot stop the smile that spreads across my face, almost regretting that he is unable to see it behind my mask before I slam him back down to the ground.

He lays in a crumpled mess at my feet, gasping for breath and unable to move.

I prepare myself to do what I must.

To finally end him.

I cannot lie and say that I will not take great pleasure in this moment, especially as understanding fills his eyes.

Yet, before I can do anything, the room suddenly fills with the echo of approaching guards. I reach for Hades just as vines shoot from the floor, wrapping around me and rooting me to the spot.

I let out an annoyed hiss as I turn to look toward the door as Persephone steps into the room, anger on her face as she glances between her husband and me.

"That will be enough."

I spit out a curse, struggling uselessly against her vines as one I tear through is instantly replaced with another.

"I said enough," Persephone snaps.

Hades, who has now managed to get to his feet, whirls on her.

Anger flashing in his eyes as he stares her down, but she does not cower under the weight of his rage.

Not even as he takes a threatening step toward her. He seems ready to take her down, but stops as Eros moves to stand in the doorway, Cerberus at his side and another figure just behind him.

Anteros.

Frowning, I ask, "What is the meaning of this?"

Persephone's lip curls up as she glances between all of us. After a moment she steps to the side, motioning for Anteros to come forward.

The man does, looking more annoyed and inconvenienced than anything as he takes in the scene before him.

"I have been summoned to oversee a trial," he announces, his tone almost sounding offended.

I narrow my eyes at this.

There is only one trial that involves him, and it is not one any of us would be foolish enough to ever evoke, one that all of us know better than to breathe a word of.

"For who?" I ask, knowing this is unlikely to end well for anyone involved.

"A mortal by the name of Hazel," Anteros says.

"What," I breathe, my entire body tensing as my heart skips a beat in my chest. "Who the hell would call for such a thing?"

"I did," Eros says.

My eyes narrow as I stare at the man. Without meaning to, I rip through the vines holding me in place and take a menacing step toward him. The idiot has gone too far this time.

"You fool, what have you done?!"

Raising his hands in defense, Eros is quick to say, "Wait, let me explain."

"Speak," I snarl. "Before I tear your head from your shoulders."

"As is one of my rights as brother to Anteros, I did not call it for myself," he pauses for a second before continuing, "but for you."

HAZEL

I have no idea what's happening, or what this trial they speak of is.

From my place on Hades' bed, with the sheets now clutched to me, I watch as Death tenses. If his reaction is anything to go by, I'm not sure I *want* to know.

Death seems furious as he tears at the vines, freeing himself enough to march toward Eros. Wincing, I wait for another fight to break out.

But before he can reach Eros, Death is stopped by Anteros and Persephone stepping into his path.

"The trial has already been called for," Anteros says. "It must be carried out."

"She is in no condition to undergo such a thing," Death says.

I can feel the weight of their gazes as everyone's eyes suddenly shift toward me.

Persephone's face is hard as her eyes meet mine, and my cheeks burn with all the attention. Especially given the fact I'm currently curled up in the king's bed, my nightgown torn and my body bruised and broken.

Hugging the sheet to me as tight as I can, I wish it were possible for me to disappear entirely, as Hades did earlier. I would not blame Persephone for ending my life here and now for finding me in her husband's bed.

But as she stares at me and her eyes move across my bloodstained body, her face softens slightly.

"I understand your concerns, Death," Persephone says softly, "but the trial must be held at dawn, as is the way."

"Persephone—"

"However, I will allow you to choose someone to care for her well-being in the meantime," the queen adds. "You may remove her from the room so that I may tend to my husband."

Hades shifts at this, pulling my wary attention to him. It takes a moment for him to pull himself to his full height. Though his ego seems to have been bruised, his rage burns ever brighter in the depths of his eyes.

And I realize this trial, whatever it is, is all that has spared our lives for the time being.

The vines fall from Death's body as he turns toward me.

My heart pounds in my chest as he bends to wrap me in the silk sheets before gently lifting me into his arms. His familiar, icy touch is a welcome relief, though I still flinch in pain as he tucks me to his chest.

As we pass Persephone, I can't help but shift forward as I try to catch her attention.

"Persephone," I plead, "I swear nothing happened. I did not come here of my own choosing."

Her eyes do not lift to meet mine, but I see the way her lips press into a firm line ... and I have to hope she heard me, whether or not she believes a word I say.

As we move toward the open doorway, a wave of relief washes over me to be leaving it behind, even if I'm now to be faced with whatever strange trial awaits.

"Enjoy your last moments with your mortal, Death," Hades calls out. "The second this trial is over ... I swear on my very existence that I will make her mine."

Death does not respond, his eyes focused forward as Cerberus and Eros step aside to allow him to pass between them.

A pair of guards appear to lead us through the halls, their wary distance a strange comfort as we walk. Death is tender in his touch, trying his hardest not to jostle me in his arms.

Still, I wince in pain.

Try as I might, I cannot seem to find my voice, let alone the words to tell Death how much I've missed him.

But my tongue refuses to obey, and my heart still pangs with worry over his honesty in regard to our deal.

So, instead, I savor the frosty smell of him, the concern in his eyes each time they glance down to check on me.

The guards lead us to a small room, barely large enough for a bed and a small table, with a single window high up on the wall. It's more akin to a prison cell than anything else, and still far too close to Hades for my comfort, but it would appear we have no choice.

Death seems reluctant as he sets me down gently on the bed, taking care not to jar my broken body any more than necessary. Pain flares up at even the slightest touch, and I can barely stifle the whimper that escapes my lips.

Our eyes meet for a moment before he straightens, a thousand unspoken words passing between us. But then he moves away without either of us giving voice to any of them, and I'm left biting my lip, unsure how to break the silence between us.

As Death steps out of the room, Eros appears at his side, a look passing between the two of them.

"Take care of her," Death says softly.

Eros nods.

Shifting forward slightly as I ask, "Where ... where is he going?"

Frowning at the phrasing of my question.

"Tell her what you can," Death says, again addressing Eros as a second strange look passes between them. "Until the trial."

I'm even more unsettled by this trial now than I was before.

What isn't he telling me? Why won't he speak to me himself?

But before I can open my mouth to try to press the issue, several guards step forward, and I watch in dismay as he's led away from the room.

Anteros moves to stand in the doorway, a bored expression on his face as he watches Death being escorted away. The first glimmer of emotion flickers across his face as he turns back to Eros.

"Need I remind you, brother, not to interfere with the rules of the trial?" Anteros asks Eros.

"No," Eros says with a deep sigh.

"Good," his brother says, handing him a small box. "Then you know what is expected of you."

Without waiting for his brother's response, Anteros ushers him into the room. Closing the door softly behind him, I am left alone with Eros.

After a pause, Eros turns to me. He winces as if sensing my pain and I'm reminded of the cuts that cover me, and the glass that's still embedded in a number of them.

Though the pain is still there, it is little more than a dull throb ... so long as I sit still.

"Here, let me try to help you," Eros says, crossing to set the small box on the table beside the bed. I say nothing as he opens it and begins pulling out various items.

"What is this trial, Eros?" I ask, flinching at how unsubtle my question is. "What am I supposed to do?"

Eros doesn't answer as he comes to crouch before me. I frown, chewing my lip in thought as I try to puzzle out how to get him to talk to me about it.

Silence fills the room as he wets a bit of clean cloth with something from a small vial. Pressing it to a cut, a hiss of pain escapes me. He gives me a soft look before pressing slightly harder.

"Am I going to face Death in the trial?"

Again, he says nothing, this time giving me a look that practically begs me to stop with the questions.

"Is there some larger purpose behind this trial? What does a Trial of Love entail? Eros, please."

His continued silence grates on me, and I can't understand why he refuses to answer my questions ...

Until it dawns on me that he may not be allowed to speak of the trial.

"You can't tell me about it can you?"

He shakes his head.

Of course.

Frustration washes over me as I press my lips together.

Carefully, he sets about cleaning the rest of my wounds. He's surprisingly gentle as he pulls the glass from my wounds.

The silence between us stretches on, broken only by the soft sounds of Eros working. I can't help but wonder what he's thinking, what he's feeling.

As he finishes cleaning the last of my cuts, he stands and starts to turn away. I reach out for him, catching his wrist, and he freezes.

"What's wrong, Eros?"

Slowly, he turns to look at me, his expression pained.

"I am sorry."

"For what?"

He lets out a heavy sigh.

"For getting you into this mess. I should have known better than to even suggest sending you to the ball to seduce Hades. I should have—"

"Stop." His eyes widen slightly as I cut him off. "This is my own doing. My own choices led me here. I am the one who was foolish enough to make a deal with Death. I should have known better than to believe I could take fate into my own hands."

Eros shifts uncomfortably at this. Narrowing my eyes,

I watch him for a moment, but even in his blindness he won't quite meet my gaze.

"What is it, Eros?"

He hesitates for a moment before saying, "You should know how much it pains me to say this. Truly, I hate to even mention this, but I have never known Death to take payment for a deal and *not* fulfill his side of the bargain."

"What?" the word barely makes it past my lips as my breath catches in my throat.

"All I am saying is that—"

"You can't be serious," I snap as I'm reminded of Death's broken promise. "You saw my father's soul on the other side of the gates."

"You were right that he should not have died so soon. But how can you be so sure that Death broke his side of the deal?"

I open my mouth to answer this before blinking.

Slowly, I close my mouth.

My heart skips as I consider what Eros is suggesting. Is it really possible that despite our deal, despite my bargaining, my father still met an untimely end?

"Is that really possible?"

Eros shrugs, but it's enough to plant a seed of doubt in my mind.

My heart races as I consider this.

I can't help but reflect on everything I've said and done since seeing my father's soul at the gates.

At the harsh words I snapped at Death, and the way I was too quick to rush into Eros's arms.

And yet, despite all of that, he still came for me when I needed him the most.

A lump begins to form in my throat as tears mist my eyes.

"What am I to do?" I ask Eros.

He gives me a gentle smile as he settles on the edge of the bed and reaches for me.

I let him gather me in his arms, rocking me softly as he runs a hand through my hair. Offering me comfort when I need it the most.

"Listen to your heart," he says, his voice all too gentle and soothing. "When you face what is to come."

I glance up at him, just as he presses a palm to my cheek.

The next thing I know, he's bent his lips to mine, stopping just short of kissing me. He remains frozen there for a moment, before quickly pulling away, a curse on his lips as he puts distance between us.

"What's wrong?"

He shakes his head.

"I am sorry, Hazel. I have to go."

"Why?"

He opens his mouth but then forces it closed. His expression hardens as he stares down at me.

A question forms and dies on my lips just as the door swings open and Anteros strides into the room.

He nods at Eros.

"It is time."

Without so much as another word or further explanation, Eros offers his hand to me. I take it, allowing him to help me to my feet.

As soon as I am standing, he drops my hand and steps away, as if he can no longer stand to touch me. As he moves to exit the room, his brother stops him to lean in and whisper something.

Eros looks surprised, but then nods.

I frown after him, wondering what was just said, as he strides silently from the room. Anteros watches after him for a long moment before looking back to me.

Motioning to several guards, they lead me from the room.

HAZEL

Not a single word is spoken between us as I'm escorted through the palace and out into the city.

I was beginning to think I would only ever know the four walls of Hades' castle, and I can't help the way my heart leaps with joy as we put it behind us. But as we move deeper into the City of the Gods, I realize that my excitement may be short-lived.

Leaving Hades' palace may not have been such a good thing after all.

The streets are already lined with spectators.

Their eyes bore into me as I'm led past them. I can hear their whispering, laughter, and jeers, but none of it makes any sense to me. Most seem to be celebrating which only makes me warier as I'm led to a part of the city that I've yet to step foot in.

The crowd only thickens here, the faces all blurring together as the creatures of the Underworld jostle one another for the chance to look upon me.

A large arena made of bright white stone looms ahead of us, and I can't help but stare up at it, craning my neck back to make out the shining golden top of it.

It's stunning, the delicate columns and stones begging to find themselves captured by a paintbrush. My fingers twitch in a way I'd almost forgotten at the thought, and for just a moment I allow myself to be distracted.

Panic is quick to overcome any daydreams about painting though as Anteros leads me into the arena. I barely manage to catch a glimpse of the beautiful marble floors as I'm led to a small room.

"You will await further instructions here," Anteros tells me.

Heavy metal bars fall over the doorway, efficiently trapping me alone in the room. I watch as he moves away, the guards leaving with him.

Turning back to look around the empty space, I let out a sigh.

There's not much to do here but wait and wonder about what's about to happen.

Will I find myself standing before the Judges? Or perhaps this is a trial for some crime they believe I have committed against love?

I suppose anything is possible. Here, I'm starting to think anything is possible, but the more I try to imagine what I'm about the face, the faster my heart begins to race.

Unable to stand still, I begin to pace as my mind runs wild.

"Hazel."

Blinking, it takes a moment to pull myself from my

thoughts as I turn to find Cerberus standing at the gates, watching me with concern in his eyes.

"What are you doing here?" I ask as I frown at him.

I'm still too anxious and overwhelmed by my thoughts to want to deal with him right now.

"Please," he whispers, "we do not have much time."

The urgency in his voice breaks through to me, and I have no choice but to step toward him.

"What is it?" I ask, something about his face and voice making me realize that I should listen to him.

He shifts forward, slipping his hand through the bars. Opening his palm, I stare at the small piece of paper that lies there.

I eye it warily for a moment before quickly reaching to take it.

Only he closes his hand before I can grab it, catching me in his grip. I glare up at him.

"What kind of trick is this?"

"It is no trick," he rushes to say. "I will give you the note, but I would like to ask your forgiveness for not doing a better job of protecting you."

I blink at him in surprise.

"I do not think this is an appropriate time to be having this conversation."

His gaze drops, and I almost think that I see a single tear slip down his cheek. Frowning, I shift closer but when he meets my gaze, I swear his cheeks are dry.

"You are right, of course," he says, releasing his hold on me.

The parchment in hand, I turn my back to the door.

Opening the note, I inhale sharply at the small illustrated page that was torn out of the book Cyprian gave me ... and on it, in Cyprian's own handwriting is one word.

Nightshade.

I stare at the word for a long moment, my mind spinning. Then, with horror, I stumble back. The pungent scent that filled Father's room when he lay ill.

It hits me all at once, nearly choking the air from me. The memory is so strong, I swear I almost find myself standing back in his room that day.

Of course, at the time, it had been masked by so many other scents that I hadn't immediately been able to pinpoint it.

But now, it's clear as day.

The smell that haunts me slowly dissipates as I realize what it means.

Father was poisoned.

Is this Death's way of proving to me that someone else killed my father?

If so, then it means that despite my best efforts, even our deal would not have saved him from an untimely death.

Not if his murderer still lived.

Whirling, I turn back to Cerberus, questions at the ready. Only the space beyond the bars is empty.

I open my mouth, not sure if I can summon him back or not, but a startled sound comes out instead just as the groan of metal grinding together fills the small space.

Turning to look at the far wall, I watch as it slowly

gives way to the arena floor beyond. Blinking, I stare out at the space just as my name is called.

Taking a deep breath, I clutch the note in the palm of my hand ... and then step toward the arena and whatever trial awaits me within.

DEATH

I make my way into the arena, my guard on high as I pause before the large gate that leads to the main area.

My eyes move about as I take it in. A simple open space, meant for soldiers to show off their fighting skills.

Above it, a crowd of gods and monsters have already filled the stands, watching and waiting for the trial to begin.

Though I know what is to be tested, I have no idea *how* I will be tested. That alone is enough to have me on edge. I cannot begin to imagine what Hazel must be thinking and feeling right now as she faces this.

Alone and unprepared.

Setting my jaw, I step into the arena.

Immediately, my mind goes blank. The space before me transforms before my eyes and I blink twice to make my vision focus.

I am home.

Frowning, I take a step as I try to recall where I have been.

But I have no recollection of where I have been or who I even am ... or *what* I am.

All I know is this moment of stepping into my home having returned from a long journey.

Something warms my hand and I glance down in surprise to find a small glass vial, devoid of any substance, held in the palm of my hand.

I frown at it.

Why would I be holding such a thing?

Shaking my head, I move further into my palace.

I reach the cold fireplace and set the vial atop the mantel, staring at it for a moment.

I cannot for the life of me remember why I would have such a thing, but then my attention falls to the fireplace.

It bothers me that there is no fire lit within.

But why?

This has never bothered me before; I like things cold and dark and empty.

At least, I thought I did.

Now, I am suddenly not so sure of anything.

Confused, I reach for the vial again. It seems wrong to leave it here above the cold fireplace. Instead, I tuck it into my pocket before turning to go about my normal daily tasks.

Walking through the palace halls, an odd feeling comes over me.

My eyes keep noting the empty walls. The dusty kitchen. The clean floors.

I cringe at the lone echo of each step I take.

It is as if there is something missing. As if something deeply important to me has been taken from me without my knowledge.

But what?

I pause in a hallway, glancing about the empty space.

It feels so lifeless here.

But that should not bother me. So, why is it?

I set off again only to abruptly stop again.

Slowly, I turn toward a door that I never use and throw it open.

The space beyond is empty, just as I expected.

And yet, I know there used to be something here. Something terribly valuable. Of that, I am sure.

But I simply cannot remember what.

No matter how hard I search my mind, I come up empty. My mind nothing but a blank canvas unwilling to be painted.

Frustrated, I leave the room and storm toward my bedchamber.

I throw open the door before moving toward the mirror. Leaning closer I stare at my maskless reflection.

I blink.

Startled, I realize that I am seeing my unmasked face, and then my eyes shift toward the bed.

My heart pangs as my gut twists.

Whirling I stare at the bed and the woman lying there. Her blonde hair halos her face, her curvy figure barely concealed beneath the silken sheets of my bed.

Unable to stop myself, I take a step toward her.

The woman's eyes flutter open and she smiles sweetly up at me.

"Welcome home," her soft voice greets me.

I frown down at her.

Who is this woman?

She laughs and I realize I have asked the question out loud.

"I am your wife," she tells me. "What a silly question. Now, come to bed. I have missed you terribly."

I shake my head, taking a step back. Suddenly all I want is to put as much distance between us as possible.

"No, I have business to attend to," I say, the excuse bubbling from my lips before I can stop it.

She pouts prettily, shifting in a way I am sure is meant to convince me to join her in bed.

Yet, I am not tempted.

There is something wrong here, though I cannot put my finger on it.

"Very well," she finally says. "Will you at least see to it that the children are taken care of?"

"Children?"

She lets out an annoyed sigh at this. "How is it that you can pretend to have forgotten your own children too?"

Anger fills her face, and I do my best to placate it with promises of checking that the children are fine. Even as I search my mind for the faces of these supposed children of mine and come up empty.

Sweeping from the room, I make my way through the palace, my shadows sweeping up around me in agitation.

Slipping my hand into my pocket as I walk, lost in

trying to solve the puzzle of the woman in my bed and the children she speaks of, my fingers absently wrap around the vial.

A jolt of heat shoots up my arm at the contact, and I stop and pull the vial out.

Frowning, I turn it over in my hand.

The is vial now partially full with a thick golden liquid.

Something familiar seeps into my mind as I stare at it. Only just as an image starts to form in my mind, laughter pulls my attention away from the vial.

Pocketing it again, I move toward the sound.

I push open a door, finding three children sitting on the floor surrounded by toys. The blonde woman sits amongst them, smiling sweetly as she watches them play.

I cannot miss the way the children look like perfect blends of the woman and myself.

Watching them for a moment, I cannot help but take a step into the room. Drawn by the warmth of the scene before me.

The children turn to me, smiling and laughing as they leap to their feet and race toward me.

At the last second, I take a step back. Stopping them from reaching me or coming any closer. I shake my head as my eyes narrow on the woman.

This is not right.

She stands, her face upset.

"You are acting like a beast," she tells me. "Unable to greet your wife and then not even hugging your children? Is this the sort of monster I married?"

I shake my head, turning and striding from the room.

My mind spins.

This is not right.

This is not my home.

She ... they are not my family.

I let my feet carry me through my palace until I find myself nearly to the Valley of Death. Without hesitation, I traverse the dense fog until I step into the golden fields.

Knax comes prancing toward me and I smile at him as he nuzzles me in welcome. I savor the moment, finally something that feels right.

As it should be.

After a minute, I pull myself atop Knax. With a click of my tongue, we race off. Away from my palace and my realm, and into the realm of the mortals.

I do not know where I am going, or if I even have a destination in mind.

But I feel drawn here.

I push Knax faster and faster, suddenly filled with eagerness to reach the end of our journey. I have a feeling something awaits me at the end.

Something true. Something real.

Finally, we come to a stop just outside a manor tucked away on a hill.

Dismounting, I stride toward the front door and throw it open.

Only, as I step through, I suddenly find myself in a huge arena.

HAZEL

I'm wary as I step into the arena.

A strange quiet settles over it, and I can't help but feel on edge until I see Death standing in the very center.

My heart skips a beat as a smile pulls at my lips.

I move to hurry toward him, but my steps falter when I realize that we are not alone.

Stepping from the shadows that are now slowly creeping closer all around us, is Hades.

I stop in my tracks, my stomach dropping at the sight of him. A slow smile pulls at the corners of the king's mouth as he stares at me for a long moment before glancing toward Death.

It's only now that I realize Death seems to be lost in a daze, unaware of my presence.

Hades raises a hand and I follow his gesture as I look up at the audience that fills the stands high above us. Their eyes all seem to be fixed on me, despite Hades and Death standing not far off.

"For her trial, she must simply make a choice," Hades announces.

He motions to the far side of the arena, and I turn to watch Cerberus enter the arena. Next to him is a man, his head bowed as he's half-held and half-dragged to stand next to Hades.

It's only as they step into the center of the slowly dimming light that I realize the man with Cerberus is familiar.

More than familiar.

The man standing before me, his head bowed as Hades gestures to Cerberus to lift it for us all to see his face, is my father.

Tears sting my eyes as I glance back at Hades, and he grins widely at me.

"My trial, what is it?" I ask.

Hades nods slowly.

"Yours is a simple one. All you must do is choose, mortal."

"Choose."

"Yes," he says, a wicked grin spreading across his face. "You must choose between saving your father or saving Death."

I blink as I consider this, my eyes slowly slipping to Death for a moment. He stands strangely still, a blank look on his face as he gazes out at the crowd. As though he's unaware that I'm here.

"If you choose Death," Hades continues. "Then your father's soul will move on to the afterlife."

I consider this for a moment before asking, "And if I choose my father?"

"Death will cease to exist as you know him."

Blinking, I realize what a strangely vague answer that is. It certainly doesn't give me much to go on.

Though perhaps that's the reason it's worded so.

"Please," I say. "Don't make me choose between them. Instead, take my life and allow them both to keep theirs."

"No. That is not the choice you have been given, mortal."

"Please."

"You must choose between your father or Death. There is no third option here."

Biting my lip, I try in vain to keep the tears in my eyes from spilling over. I fail as I glance between my father and Death.

It's an impossible choice, either way, guilt is sure to wreak havoc on me for the rest of my life. How am I meant to choose between two souls I care so deeply for?

"Make your choice, mortal," Hades says. "Your time runs short."

My heart shatters in my chest as my eyes move between the two men before me.

I try to reason with myself as I sort through the choice I have to make. I came here to save my father.

Everything I have done so far has been for him.

But can I continue down that path if another's existence is now at risk?

It was one thing to give my life for his, but it is quite another to bargain with Death's, to offer up his very existence in exchange for my father's soul.

Closing my eyes, I take a deep breath as I give myself

a moment to try and calm the storm of pain and sorrow that has arisen within me.

My hand clenches, the note softly crinkling in my palm.

And I know my answer.

DEATH

All of a sudden, everything comes sharply into focus, and I see a girl standing before me. Tears staining her cheeks as she stares at me. My heart pounds as I stare back at her.

Somehow, I know that *she* is the one I am looking for.

She is my missing piece.

My everything.

I watch her as she pulls herself up tall, wiping the tears from her cheeks. I listen as Hades repeats the choice being given to her, and my heart breaks for her.

I would do anything for her.

Anything to ease the pain of this moment.

Anything to protect her heart and soul from the devastation that comes with making such a choice.

And I will.

Setting my jaw, I force my feet to carry me forward.

I push past Hades and move toward her father. He glances up at me, his eyes blank and unseeing as I come to a stop before him.

Instead of forcing her to choose, I reach out.

In a blink, I surrender my immortal powers into her father's body.

A gasp escapes me as I feel the very essence of my being begin to drain from me.

A cold more painful than anything I have experienced wraps around me ... but for a strange warmth that seems to come from my pocket.

Reaching in I pull out a completely full vial, the golden liquid within glowing warmly as I stare at it.

Suddenly, it shatters in my palm the liquid oozing out and up my hand to slip beneath my sleeve.

I cry out as it burns into my skin, wrapping its way up my arm and across my chest before finally burrowing its way into my heart.

I gasp, and in an instant, my memories return in a rush.

"Little one," I breathe.

My heart and mind are overcome with her.

Turning, my eyes find her one last time just before my vision grows dark.

"Death!"

My name on her lips is the last thing I hear as my heart and mind go still. Peace fills me, my shadows pooling around me as I fall to my knees.

Smiling softly to myself, I know that I have given her my all.

My soul.

My heart.

My very existence.

She is and always will be my everything, and I have finally proved it beyond a shadow of a doubt.

I have loved her as only I could ...

Until death.

THANK YOU

Thank you for reading *Until Death*, the third book in the *Tempting the Fates* series.

If you enjoyed this book ...

You can stay up to date on upcoming new releases in this series and others by following Alice Wilde on **Amazon**, **Facebook**, Instagram, or Tiktok, or by signing up for her newsletter at alicewilde.com.

If you would recommend this book, or others by Alice Wilde, please consider leaving a review on Amazon or reaching out to let her know!

Pack Lies

Pack Mates

Pack Alpha

The Royal Shifters

Her Betrothal

Her Highlander

Her Viking

Her Warrior

Her Prophecy

The Shifters of Africa

The Lioness of Egypt

The Pride of Egypt

The Queen of Egypt

Quick Reads

My Cup of Tea

The Christmas Wish

ABOUT THE AUTHOR

Alice Wilde works as a full-time game editor, graphic designer, and, most importantly, author.

She loves creating paranormal, fantasy romances full of gorgeous men, magic, twists, and cliffhangers that she hopes her readers enjoy reading as much as she enjoys writing them.

Alice currently lives in Asia with her cat dreaming up, writing down, and living in her next book alongside her characters ...

Follow Alice Wilde on Facebook/ Amazon to stay up to date with new releases.

Connect with Alice

Email: **alicewildeauthor@gmail.com**

Tiktok: @aliceWildeauthor

 facebook.com/AliceWildeAuthor

 instagram.com/alice_wilde_author

Printed in Great Britain
by Amazon

30309461R00144